Will   Irma   Taranee   Cornelia   Hay Lin

Enchanted Waters

Adapted by **ALICE ALFONSI**

HYPERION PAPERBACKS FOR CHILDREN
New York

W.I.T.C.H. Will Irma Taranee Cornelia Hay Lin is a trademark of Disney Enterprises, Inc. Hyperion Paperbacks for Children is an imprint of Disney Children's Book Group, L.L.C.

Printed in the United States of America
First Edition
1 3 5 7 9 10 8 6 4 2

This book is set in 12/16.5 Hiroshige Book.
ISBN-13: 978-1-4231-0289-2
ISBN-10: 1-4231-0289-4
Visit www.clubwitch.com

ONE

Stepping out of the Heatherfield police station, Irma took a deep breath of fresh air, relieved to be outside again.

For the last hour, she'd been sitting in the station's stuffy lobby, waiting to get a ride home from her dad. But it had taken him forever to leave! Earlier, he'd led a big arrest down by the Heatherfield docks and brought in a gang of very bad dudes. They'd made a lot of trouble while they were being processed.

I could have taken all of them on myself, Irma mused, but I would have had to transform, and then half the station—including my dad!—would have figured out that I was no ordinary girl. They would have seen that I was the water Guardian!

Irma ran her fingers through her short brown hair as her dad came up and signaled that it was time to go. Following him out the door and down the concrete steps of the police station, her thoughts drifted back to the strange events that had occurred only a few minutes earlier— including her run-in with a real-life criminal!

As much as the threats made by the now arrested thug had bothered her, Irma had been even more disturbed by the mysterious stranger who had seemed to know all about her and her friends. He'd called her the queen of water. Did he somehow know her secret identity?

Outside, the sun had sunk low in the sky, and shadows stretched across the line of police cars parked on the street. When they reached her dad's cruiser, Irma expected him to unlock the doors and slide behind the wheel. Instead, he just stood there, leaning against the vehicle.

"Dad!" Irma said, pulling impatiently on the locked door handle.

"We need to wait a minute," he told her.

Irma noticed that his gaze was fixed on the entrance to the police station, and she looked over. Two officers were leading a prisoner through the front doors and down the steps.

The prisoner was tall and nicely dressed. He wore pressed slacks and an expensive-looking sweater. One police officer held his right arm. Another held his left; together, they shuffled the man toward a police wagon.

From a distance, the prisoner looked more like a banker than a criminal; only the handcuffs he wore gave away his status. It seemed wrong to Irma that he was being treated so rudely. When the suspect got closer, however, Irma understood why he was handcuffed.

The man's facial expression was twisted and full of rage. Long black sideburns hugged his flushed face. His lean body was tense; he was resisting the officers. And his eyes were darker and colder than storm clouds.

As he passed Irma's dad, the man sneered with ferocity. "We'll meet again, cop," he said.

The man's hard voice sent a chill through Irma. "Dad," she whispered as the officers pulled the man farther away, "am I wrong, or was that guy threatening you?"

Irma's dad looked down at her and smiled. "Mark Zibosky barks, but he never bites," he said calmly.

Irma wasn't so sure. As the man, Zibosky, was loaded into the back of the police wagon, his stare never left her father's face. He looked more than capable of biting.

I know my dad's job is dangerous, Irma thought. He deals with criminals every day. But this guy's obviously no *everyday* criminal!

Irma opened her mouth to ask another question about Zibosky, but her dad held up his hand. "Let's change the subject, okay?" His firm tone made it clear he didn't want to talk about Zibosky any further.

"Okay," Irma said, pushing Zibosky's scary gaze out of her mind. After all, coming to the police station wasn't Irma's typical after-school routine. She'd come as a favor to her father, bringing some files he needed from home. Seeing a criminal had not been part of the plan. So she was more than willing to forget about everything she had seen . . . if she could.

"So tell me," she said, changing the subject, "what are we still hanging around out here for?"

"We're waiting for company," her dad replied. "And here he comes now!"

Irma followed the direction of her dad's gaze and saw an elderly man exiting the police station. He wore a tattered, sea green overcoat, and his long white hair flowed out from under a navy blue knit cap. Irma recognized him right away. He was the same guy she'd talked to inside the station house earlier.

Walking closely beside the man was Rose, an officer who worked with Irma's dad. Rose was slender, with long brown hair, which she wore in a single, thick braid down her back. She was also a little shy—and sometimes she tended to stammer—but her martial arts moves were totally awesome, as she had proved back inside not too long ago.

Irma watched Rose lead the old man down the front steps of the station, through the parking area, and right over to Irma's dad.

"H—he's all yours, T—Tom!" Rose said. Then she added, "C—could you still give me that ride you offered?"

"Sure thing, Rose," Irma's dad replied, finally unlocking his police car.

Rose helped the old man into the backseat. Then Irma's dad said, "Irma, would you mind sitting in back with Mr. Jewell?"

Irma's eyes widened in alarm. She glanced through the back window at the man she now knew as Mr. Jewell. Sure, she had shared a bench with the guy inside the police station. She'd even offered him a cup of water from the cooler. But that was as friendly as she wanted to get!

Being nice to a prisoner was one thing, she thought. Being trapped in the backseat of a car with him was something else!

"Um, isn't that the old guy who was just wearing handcuffs?" Irma asked her father softly. She noticed he was no longer wearing them, which worried her even more!

"Don't worry," Irma's dad replied with a laugh. "During today's roundup, there was some confusion."

Irma frowned. If this guy's any part of Mark Zibosky's gang, she thought, then he's got to be a three-alarm hazard!

Her dad continued, "It seems that Jewell was Zibosky's *victim*, and not an accomplice."

"Poor guy," Rose added. "Those th—thugs had him locked up in a dark, damp cellar."

"Yep. They told us he's some kind of fortune-teller." Irma's dad smiled. "What do you think of that?"

"A fortune-teller?" Irma mumbled under her breath. "I think it's weird. That's what I think."

To herself, she added, *but it does kind of make sense. He does know an* awful *lot about me.*

Her dad lowered his voice, interrupting her thoughts. "He doesn't talk much, but he seems like a nice guy. I think he's homeless. That's why we're taking him downtown to the local shelter. It's on our way home."

Irma's dad held the door open for her, effectively putting an end to any more conversation about Jewell. She slid into the backseat, beside the old man. Taking a closer look, it was easy to believe Jewell was homeless. His coat was worn and patched at the elbows. His gloves were frayed, and the tops of the fingers were cut off.

Irma awkwardly waved at the man. *What do you say in a situation like this?* she asked herself. *Um . . . pleased to meet you. So nice to know you're not a dangerous criminal like I thought you were.*

Yeah, she thought, *that'll be sure to break the ice!*

"Er . . . hi, there!" Irma blurted out instead. She gritted her teeth in an uneasy grin. "We meet again!"

Jewell responded with a gentle smile. His skin was wrinkly and nut brown, as if he'd weathered the elements for years. He had bushy white eyebrows and a large nose with a crook in the bridge. He didn't seem mean, like Zibosky. He seemed friendly and kind.

Up front, Irma's father climbed behind the wheel, while in the passenger seat next to him, Rose nervously pushed up her square red glasses. Irma's dad glanced over at his colleague.

"Rose," he said, "have I congratulated you on how you immobilized those three guys in the station?"

"J—just r—routine administration," Rose stammered.

Irma smiled at the woman's response. Rose was obviously proud of having single-handedly taken out a few bad guys. And she was probably itching to do it again.

Irma knew exactly how she felt. Of course, Irma and her four best friends—Will, Taranee, Cornelia, and Hay Lin—usually fought dark forces and supernatural creatures, not everyday thugs. But Irma figured the feeling of stopping them was just as satisfying.

"You were fantastic," Irma's dad gushed to Rose. He started the cruiser and pulled out of the parking area. "Phil Shepard was really impressed."

"Ph—Phil?" Rose repeated. Her pale skin blushed pink as a flower petal. "Oh, come on. You're j—just saying that b—because you know I like him!"

Irma's dad shook his head. "I'm saying it because it's true! That self-defense book you were talking about is really working!"

"Not self-defense. Self-*esteem*," Rose said, correcting him. "Y—you want to hear about it?"

"Sure," said Irma's father.

Rose cleared her throat. "W—well, the f—first chapter says that . . ."

Irma listened for a few minutes as Rose discussed overcoming her shyness—something Irma had never had a problem with. In fact, her problem—or so her friends told her—was the exact opposite.

Whenever Irma had a thought, it usually leaped right out of her mouth. And *usually* she got away with it. But sometimes, her friends got on her case about her all-too frequent outbursts—like when she'd started singing the song "Mandy," for example, in front of Will.

Talk about something really not going over well, Irma thought, cringing at the memory.

Will's crush, Matt Olsen, had written the song a long time ago to play with his band, Cobalt Blue. The song was all about Mandy Anderson, his first love. *Mandy, sweet as candy, you're my first love, and you send me above . . .*

Matt and Mandy were just friends now. They hadn't been girlfriend and boyfriend in years. Unfortunately, Will hadn't been aware of that when she first learned about Mandy (from her astral drop, no less!), and Matt had never had the chance to explain the situation. So it was still a touchy subject, and any mention of the name Mandy had the ability to shatter her totally.

Of course, Irma hadn't thought of that when she'd started to sing the song in front of Will outside their school one day not too long before.

And that obviously wasn't the first time Irma had blurted something out without thinking. While the other girls usually tolerated it, Cornelia tended to get annoyed more easily. In Irma's opinion, however, Cornelia herself could be a real pain.

It's not surprising Corny's the earth

Guardian, Irma thought. Her head's rock hard, and her attitude's stiffer than stone!

But, no matter what anyone else thought, Irma liked having a big mouth. She was proud of being loud and bold and funny. That was what made her Irma! Her fearlessness also made it easy for her to talk to people . . . like back in the station house, when she'd offered Jewell a cup of water.

I never have a problem talking to people, she thought. So why am I suddenly clamming up now? What's wrong with me?

She glanced over at Jewell. Well . . . I guess he does make me kind of nervous, she thought, but still, I feel like I know him. There's something so familiar about him.

Jewell's head was turned sideways as he looked out the car window; Irma took advantage of his distraction to examine him more closely. She noticed he was holding a red book in his arms, and hugging it to his chest.

Just then, he turned and stared right at her. Beneath his bushy white eyebrows, his eyes shone brighter than shimmering blue water.

His gaze is so . . . deep, Irma thought.

"Like the sea," Jewell said.

"Huh? Wh—what?" Irma blurted out, her own blue eyes growing wide with surprise. Had she spoken out loud? No, she hadn't said *anything* aloud about his eyes being deep or sealike.

"Would you lend me that red pen you've got in your pocket?" Jewell asked, nodding at the left side of Irma's coat and ignoring her surprised expression.

"I . . . um . . . sure!" she said. Without thinking, she reached inside her left pocket. "I think I have one right here in my . . ." Her fingers closed on a pen. She brought it out and froze. The pen was in the exact pocket he'd nodded toward. And it was red!

It . . . can't be, she thought. How did he know?

Irma handed the man her pen. He nodded and smiled. She watched him open the red book he'd been clutching. Then, he began to write something.

Irma swallowed uneasily. What if he really is a fortune-teller? she thought. I mean, I *have* seen stranger things! Like, weird creatures traveling to Earth from other dimensions! Or a regular girl finding out she's really the queen of another world!

Could Jewell possibly know about that, too? Irma wondered.

She closed her eyes and took a deep breath. She told herself to calm down. Maybe Jewell could read her mind. But that didn't mean he knew *all* her secrets—that Irma and her best friends were really powerful Guardians who protected the universe from evil. After all, sometimes even she found it hard to believe.

Not long ago, the girls' lives had been pretty typical. They had attended school at Sheffield Institute and spent their spare time going to the mall, talking about boys, planning parties, and hanging out.

Then something strange had happened. Each of them became aware of new abilities. Hay Lin had the power to control air. Cornelia could manipulate earth, rocks, and plants. Taranee could control fire. And Irma was able to command water.

One day, when the girls got together after school to talk about these strange new powers, Hay Lin's grandmother, Yan Lin, had walked in on them. She gave them the Heart of Candracar and basically said, "You girls have all been anointed by the Oracle of Candracar to be the new generation of Guardians. Good luck with that!"

While Will hadn't gained control over a specific element, she *had* been chosen as the Keeper of the Heart. The ancient crystal amulet had the ability to unite and magnify the powers of the other Guardians. Individually, the girls weren't exceptionally powerful. But when they worked together, they were the most awesome force in the universe! Soon after they learned their destiny, the girls had started calling themselves W.I.T.C.H., a name they'd created using their first initials.

Transforming into Guardians had some pretty odd side effects. The girls' bodies instantly matured, their limbs becoming longer and stronger. Their ordinary clothes gave way to massively cool turquoise-and-purple costumes, and they even formed wings!

Of course, the girls weren't automatically good at being Guardians. Like anything else, they had had to practice. At first they hadn't known how to control their powers, and had made a mess of things every time they tried out a new skill. Irma, for example, quickly learned that the wings on her back were for show, not real flight—but that was only after taking some pretty serious tumbles off high ledges. Hay Lin was the only one who had really been able to fly from the start. Then again, what else would one expect from an air Guardian?

Becoming powerful Guardians hadn't just changed the girls physically. Bookworm Taranee, for instance, had once been really afraid of fire. But as a Guardian, she'd had to learn how to control her fear as well as the flames.

Will, an insecure tomboy, hadn't really seemed like a natural-born leader. Everyone had assumed that Cornelia—who was the bossiest and most self-assured member of the group—would take control. So at first it felt awkward for Will to be calling the shots as Keeper of the Heart.

Eventually, however, after a number of harrowing battles that had led to a run-in with a powerful ex-Guardian named Nerissa, Will had evolved into a strong and confident Keeper.

Nerissa had been a tough force, though. She had mastered some magic that was ancient, powerful, and dark. Her goal? Attack and destroy Candracar. But she hadn't been strong enough to do that right away. After years imprisoned on a cold mountain, she had been weak. She'd needed to defeat the Guardians in order to gain more power. Then her plan was to take the Heart and use its power against the Oracle.

One of the ways Nerissa had attempted to defeat the Guardians early on had involved infiltrating their dreams. It was a very clever strategy. When the girls were awake, they could watch each other's backs. If any one of them was in trouble, the others would quickly come to her aid.

When the Guardians were alone and asleep in their bedrooms, however, they became vulnerable. Nerissa was able to enter the girls' unconscious minds and terrorize them with horrible visions.

For weeks, the girls had been plagued by the bad dreams Nerissa caused—especially Will. It had gotten so bad that they had tried to avoid sleep altogether. Soon, they were so exhausted they started dozing off in the middle of the day, only to have Nerissa's terrifying nightmares return again.

The girls had felt defeated and perplexed.

They just couldn't think of a way to fight Nerissa. But then Cornelia came up with a good idea.

The earth Guardian realized that if the girls fell asleep together in the same room, then they'd *all* be together in *one* dream. They could fight Nerissa as a team. And that was exactly what they did. Working as a team, W.I.T.C.H. defeated the evil sorceress.

Nerissa did return again, to fight another day. But by that time the girls were smarter and more experienced, and they were able to vanquish her completely, sending her to Candracar to be dealt with again by the Oracle.

Obviously, the whole Guardian experience had been extremely cosmic so far—to say the least—which was why the girls weren't really in the habit of talking with anyone about their Guardian activities.

So now, in the back of the car, Irma had to wonder . . . how had Jewell guessed at her connection to water back in the police station? When she'd brought him that cup from the cooler, he'd smiled up at her and said, "Only you could have offered me that . . . a cup of water from the queen of water." Then he'd told her that she had the power to "free" him.

Free him from what? Irma asked herself now.

This guy is probably just a little crazy, she decided. Unless . . . he really *is* a fortune-teller.

Irma wondered if she should put him to the test. All the other girls have boyfriends, she told herself. I could ask him if someday I will, too.

"I'm sorry," Jewell suddenly declared, "but I only make short-term predictions. I can't see *that* far into the future."

What does he mean *that* far? Irma automatically thought in outrage. Am I going to be single until I'm thirty or something? Then she stopped. Once again, Irma stared at Jewell in disbelief. He *must* be reading my mind, she decided. "But . . . how—"

"For now," Jewell said, "all I can tell you is that your destiny is tied to those four friends of yours."

Irma gasped. So, he *does* know about W.I.T.C.H., she realized. "But I . . . I didn't say a word!" she whispered.

Jewell closed the red book and once again hugged it to his chest. "Listen," he said urgently, "your friends all have problems that they have to overcome. You will have to help them . . . that is, if you want to help yourself."

"Help them?" Irma repeated, intrigued. "Help them *how*?"

Quietly, the man began to tell her. Irma took a deep breath, leaned forward, and listened.

TWO

Hay Lin was not happy.

At the front of the room, Mr. Collins was droning on and on about ancient Egypt. The classroom felt warm, and the air was very still. The clock on the wall seemed to grow and grow, like a timepiece from *Alice in Wonderland*. Hay Lin found herself staring at the sluggish movement of its second hand.

Tick . . . tick . . . tick . . .

Ugh, Hay Lin thought, shifting in her seat. Why couldn't we have gotten an extra hour of *art*? Why did we have to have an extra hour of *history*?

Digging into the past might have inspired an earth Guardian like Cornelia, but Hay Lin was an air Guardian. She was a free spirit, who thrived on flights of imagination. Soaring after new ideas was what excited Hay Lin—not unearthing old ones in history textbooks!

As Mr. Collins showed slide after slide of pyramids, Hay Lin felt her pretty, almond-shaped eyes closing. Her mouth began to open in a yawn and—

Wake up! she silently warned herself, snapping her mouth closed.

The last thing Hay Lin wanted to do in Mr. Collins's class was yawn. He seemed to have some sort of special yawn detector. Any student who even began to open his or her mouth instantly got called on.

Hay Lin pinched the back of her hand. She played with her blue-black pigtails. She took her magenta goggles off and put them on again.

Hay Lin liked to use her goggles as a headband. Some kids thought it was kooky. Others thought it was cool. Hay Lin, however, didn't care what *anyone* thought. If she liked how something looked, she wore it, and that was that. Like the skirt she had on today. At lunch, three girls had asked her where she'd bought it.

But she hadn't *bought* it anywhere! She'd made it.

Her favorite denim skirt had frayed at the hemline, so she'd cut off the bottom. Her hot pink dress was stained on the bodice, so she'd cut the top part away. She'd then sewn the top of her denim skirt to the ruffled bottom of her dress, and voilà—a new Hay Lin fashion statement had been born!

Fashion's way more interesting to think about than the crumbling old pyramids, Hay Lin thought as she went over the design in her head.

Tapping her chin absently, she focused on Mr. Collins's slide show. I wonder what the pyramids would look like painted in purple-and-turquoise stripes? she mused with a little smile.

"Irma!" Mr. Collins barked. "Do you know the answer?"

The history teacher's sharp voice punctured Hay Lin's fashionista fun. She turned in her seat to find Irma's blue eyes wide open in horror.

Hay Lin groaned quietly. Obviously, Irma had forgotten about Mr. Collins's yawn radar.

Irma closed her mouth and mumbled an answer.

Frowning, the history teacher shook his head, as if annoyed that Irma hadn't been paying attention. But Hay Lin knew that Irma's wrong answer was only part of the reason for his bad mood.

Mr. Collins didn't want to be teaching an extra hour of history any more than the students wanted to be learning it. He'd been forced into teaching that hour. How did Hay Lin know that? She had witnessed the whole thing earlier in the day. . . .

Walking down the hallway, Hay Lin had heard loud, angry voices. There was a pounding of fists, along with name-calling and nasty accusations. It sounded like a school-yard fight. Only it wasn't taking place outside. It was taking place in the teachers' lounge!

Curious, Hay Lin peeked through a crack in the door. The teachers were arguing about Mr. Bottlom. The computer teacher had called in sick . . . *again*. And the other teachers were tired of covering for him. No one wanted to take on an extra class, so they'd all started bickering. That was when the principal totally lost it.

"I won't tolerate fights among teachers in my school!" she declared.

Mrs. Knickerbocker was not what anyone would have called a delicate creature. She wore stiff, tailored blue suits, severe red ties, and thick glasses. Her beehive hairdo looked like an elaborate silver helmet, which had caused Irma to describe her once as a cross between a librarian and a tank.

"All right! All right!" shouted Mr. O'Neil, the tall, gruff gym teacher. "I'll stop, but only if Mr. Collins apologizes to me!"

"Apologize for what?" Mr. Collins asked, crossing his arms. "You can forget about it!"

"Gentlemen, please!" Ms. Kelly cried.

Hay Lin would have recognized the drama teacher's voice anywhere. It was so . . . *dramatic*! Ms. Kelly liked to dress dramatically, too. She always wore bold, bright gloss on her lips and some sort of flowing scarf around her neck.

Sweeping across the teachers' lounge, the drama teacher tossed her dark, curly hair and waved her hands. "Don't you realize you're fighting over something ridiculous?"

The gym teacher grunted. "We're fighting over an uncovered hour of class time, which *I* have no intention of covering!"

"Come on, O'Neil," Mr. Collins argued. "The kids would rather do an extra hour of gym than of history."

Mr. O'Neil turned to the principal in rage. "Did you hear that? He's trying to pawn this off on me!"

The principal sighed. She turned to the drama teacher. "What about you, Ms. Kelly? Aren't you free?"

Ms. Kelly's palms quickly flew up. "Absolutely not!" she exclaimed. "I've already got my hands full planning the acting seminar!"

Then the principal turned to the art teacher. "Mrs. Wharton?" she asked.

Still spying from the doorway, Hay Lin crossed her fingers. Art was one of her favorite classes. She would be more than happy to have the extra hour there!

"Sorry," Mrs. Wharton said instead— although she didn't look sorry at all. "But I have to do some still-life work with the upper-level students."

Mr. Collins stepped up to the principal. "The truth is, we can't go on covering for Bottlom."

Hearing the challenge in Mr. Collins's voice, the principal crossed her thick arms and lifted her chin. "The computer science teacher has always justified his absences."

"Yeah," griped the gym teacher, "I can imagine how. With phony doctor's notes and other ridiculous excuses."

Mr. Collins nodded and turned back to the principal. "Do you realize that a lot of the students can't even remember what his face looks like?"

Mrs. Knickerbocker tapped her chin. She paced back and forth. At last, she said, "I'll personally see to it that this unpleasant situation is resolved as soon as possible."

Mr. Collins smiled smugly. He thought he was off the hook, but he'd relaxed too soon.

"And in the meantime, Mr. Collins," the principal snapped, "take care of that uncovered hour!"

When the extra hour of history finally ended, the students shuffled toward the classroom door like zombies.

Irma was the only one who didn't walk out in a daze. Instead, she looked really upset. Hay Lin guessed that that was because of her wrong answer earlier. She followed her friend into the hall.

"Come on, Irma," she said, catching up to

her. "Collins was just being difficult. You shouldn't think anything of it."

In response, Irma exhaled, sounding like a deflating balloon. "Tell that to my dad," she said. "With the lousy grades I've been getting, I'm facing a life sentence under house arrest!"

Hay Lin put a hand on Irma's shoulder. She leaned close and lowered her voice. "So, I know we're not supposed to, but why didn't you use your powers to answer the question?"

"Sure," Irma scoffed. "It should be that easy, right?"

Hay Lin shrugged. She knew it was against the rules for the Guardians to use their powers for stuff like that, but sometimes it was okay to bend those rules a *little* bit. It wasn't going to bring the universe down! And after battling that evil sorceress Nerissa, saving Candracar, and reinstating the queen of Metamoor, Hay Lin felt that they were due for some kind of break . . . at least in school.

"The truth is, I did try," Irma admitted. "It just didn't work. I couldn't concentrate." She shook her head before adding, "Anyway, you're not going to tell the others about what I told you earlier, right?"

"I promise," Hay Lin said. "Cross my heart!" She held two fingers over her chest and crossed them.

"Good!" Irma replied. "Because Jewell made me promise I wouldn't tell anybody anything."

"Nice to know a secret's safe with you!" Hay Lin replied, biting her lip to keep from laughing. It hadn't taken very long for Irma to break her promise and spill the beans about Jewell's top secret predictions. This, Hay Lin had to admit, was fairly typical for the gossip-loving Guardian.

"So, tell me again what he said about me and my future," Hay Lin pressed as the girls strode down the crowded Sheffield Institute corridor.

"You can't really call it your future or destiny," Irma warned. "All he said was that you'd just found a new, close friend. . . ."

Hay Lin broke into a wide grin, showing off her colorful braces. "He *must* have meant Eric!" she exclaimed.

"You've also got a calm, peaceful time ahead of you," Irma added. "What's going on is nothing really major."

"That's what *you* say!" Hay Lin replied. "For me it's totally major!"

Just the thought of Eric Lyndon made Hay Lin's heart beat faster. He was Hay Lin's first crush and her first official boyfriend. He was also the coolest, cutest boy she'd ever known! He had dark, intelligent eyes and a sweet, warm smile. And he always had something interesting to say.

Eric studied astronomy with his grandfather at the Heatherfield Observatory. Before that, he'd traveled all over the world with his parents. So he knew all sorts of things. He actually spoke some Chinese—which had managed to impress even Hay Lin's parents . . . a little.

Hay Lin had met Eric the previous summer. She'd been wobbling down the street on her new Rollerblades when Eric had zoomed past her on his motor scooter. The strap of Hay Lin's handbag had caught on Eric's handlebars and . . .

CRASH!

She'd gone right down. When Eric had stopped to help her up, they'd felt an immediate connection. That evening, he'd come by her family's restaurant, the Silver Dragon, and taken Hay Lin out to the park, where they watched a meteor shower. The whole night had been so romantic!

Unfortunately, things hadn't stayed that way.

When school had started up again, Hay Lin's dreams of romantic moments in the hall and lunches together in the cafeteria were dashed. Hay Lin had begun to question Eric's feelings for her. One big reason? The school dance. Hay Lin had waited for Eric to invite her to go with him. But he never did. Instead, he acted totally awkwardly around her. It made Hay Lin feel awful, and she began to wonder if he liked some other girl.

Finally, Hay Lin had discovered the truth. Eric didn't like any other girl. It was just that he liked Hay Lin so much that he actually felt shy around her. He was *nervous* about asking her to the dance. That was why he'd kept stalling!

Now things were much better between them. Eric liked Hay Lin for who she was. He didn't care that she'd gotten braces. In fact, he thought it was cool that she had designed them herself, using W.I.T.C.H.'s elemental symbols.

Even when things got rocky, Eric had stuck by her. And it sure had gotten rocky when they went out on a double date with Taranee and her boyfriend, Nigel.

The date had started out like a dream. The two couples had gone for a stroll, hand in hand, through the twilight. City skyscrapers twinkled romantically above them. Everything seemed perfect. . . .

Then disaster struck.

As they were talking and laughing, they'd run into the nasty Uriah and his friend Kurt. One thing had quickly led to another, and things ended up getting a little physical. A bystander called the authorities. Police cars soon pulled up with sirens blaring. And Hay Lin's double date with Eric ended under the glaring, *unromantic* lights of the Heatherfield police station!

After a disaster like that, it's nice to hear Jewell's prediction, Hay Lin mused, her thoughts drifting back to Irma's news. Smooth sailing ahead sounds like major good news to me!

"To me, what he said about the others seems a lot more important," Irma said.

"That depends on your point of view," Hay Lin replied with a smile as they continued to walk down the school's main hall. "Speaking of others, there's Cornelia!"

The earth Guardian's long, blond hair was easy to spot even in crowds. It was so beautiful and lustrous that everyone else's hair looked mousy in comparison. But it was her outfits that people usually noticed first.

Shopping was Cornelia's middle name. She liked long skirts and cashmere sweaters, frilly blouses, and French berets. Her taste was usually girlish and expensive—which was why Hay Lin was surprised to see what Cornelia had on. She was wearing pinstriped orange pants that looked too big and too long—almost sloppy, compared to her normal style. And her top was basically a wide-necked T-shirt in a camouflage print.

On someone like Will, a certified tomboy, the camo T-shirt and orange pants would have been perfectly fitting. For Cornelia, however, it just seemed . . . wrong.

Something was definitely bothering Cornelia. Not only did her clothes look different, but her hair seemed kind of stringy.

It wasn't hard for Hay Lin to guess what Cornelia's problem was. In a word . . . *heartache*.

Cornelia had been the first member of W.I.T.C.H. to fall in love with a boy, and she'd fallen hard—for Caleb, a rugged young rebel she'd met in the world of Metamoor. He'd swept Cornelia into a dreamy relationship. In the end, however, that was all it turned out to be—a lovely fantasy.

Caleb had fallen in love with Cornelia when she was in her magical Guardian form. When she finally revealed her regular human self to him, Caleb had freaked. He obviously couldn't handle the reality check.

Cornelia might have been gorgeous and glamorous, but outside of her Guardian form, she was still just an ordinary human girl.

That had reminded Caleb of just how different he and Cornelia were. Caleb couldn't see himself living on Earth. And he didn't want to ask Cornelia to make a new life for herself on Metamoor. So, in the end, he broke up with her.

At first, Cornelia had cried bitterly. Then, she'd put on a brave face. Lately, however, the pain had been getting to her, and she'd been acting very moody. Some days were good. Some days were bad. And in Hay Lin's opinion, this day was clearly a bad one.

"What do I do, Hay Lin?" Irma whispered, obviously coming to the same conclusion about their friend's state of mind. "Should I tell her what Jewell said?"

Hay Lin shrugged. "If you want to get it off your chest, go ahead and tell her. But break it to her *gently*," she warned.

Irma walked up to Cornelia, who was slamming textbooks around in her metal locker. *Bam! Bam! Bam!*

"Hey, Corny!" Irma called.

Hay Lin cringed. Oh, Irma! You're already messing up, she thought. Cornelia hates that nickname!

"Um . . ." Irma continued, her face contorted into a totally forced grin. "Do you have a minute? I wanted to tell you something."

Cornelia didn't turn around. She remained seemingly fixated on the books in her locker. "Sure, Irma. I just couldn't wait to hear your voice today."

Irma cleared her throat. "Well, I . . . I think you should take up ice-skating again."

Hay Lin clasped her hands tightly and waited. When she had heard Jewell's advice for Cornelia, she'd thought it made a lot of sense.

The only question was—would Cornelia listen to the advice if it came from Irma?

"What do you care?" Cornelia asked, pulling a thick book down from her locker shelf. "You've never even seen me skate."

Irma suddenly looked very nervous, as if uncertain about what to say next. "The thing is, it's the only way that you can . . . that you can . . ."

Oh, Irma, stay cool, Hay Lin thought as she watched her friend begin to sweat.

"It's the only way that I can *what*?" Cornelia snapped.

Irma scrunched up her face. She was clearly struggling to say the next part right. Unfortunately, the water Guardian had had very little practice at being tactful!

Be careful, Irma, Hay Lin thought. Cornelia's still really, really sensitive about what happened between her and Caleb. Whatever you do, don't say anything about—

"It's the only way that you'll manage to get over your broken heart!" Irma exclaimed.

Hay Lin groaned. Anything but that! she thought. Irma had spoken so loudly that numerous kids stopped to stare at them. Cornelia turned to face Irma. Her pale skin was now red, and her usually composed features were contorted into a grimace of rage.

Irma didn't appear to notice the other kids in the hall, or Cornelia's reaction. She seemed simply relieved.

Cornelia was far from relieved. "Let me tell *you* something, Irma," she snapped.

Hay Lin shook her head. She could guess what was coming next. And she knew it wasn't going to be pretty.

Cornelia slammed her locker door shut. *BANG!* "If I *ever* decide to talk about Caleb with somebody, it certainly *won't* be with *you*! Got that?" She didn't wait for Irma to respond but spun on her heel and stormed away.

Hay Lin couldn't believe how badly that exchange had gone. Irma had royally blown it. First, she'd offended Cornelia by calling her Corny. Then she'd totally embarrassed her by practically shouting for all to hear about her friend's "broken heart"! Kids were probably already spreading rumors!

Sighing, Hay Lin moved closer to Irma. "Real smooth," she said. "I've seen elephants with more finesse than you!"

Irma sagged. "I know. I messed up," she said quietly. "But I really believe that Jewell knows what he's talking about."

Hay Lin gave another heavy sigh. When will Irma ever learn? she thought. It wasn't *what* she said. It was the *way* she said it!

Hay Lin realized that *she* had made a mistake, too. She could have prevented the whole blow-up.

After all, I know there's really only one way to control a water Guardian's mouth, she thought. Put a plug in it!

THREE

Will Vandom shut her locker door and spun the combination. Tucking the two textbooks she needed into her backpack, she was good to go.

Thank goodness homework is light tonight, she thought. I could use the break.

Will could hardly wait to get outside and feel the brisk afternoon air. Sheffield's furnace had been blasting all day, sending a ridiculous amount of heat into many of the classrooms. Math class had felt as if it were taking place in a health club sauna.

Note to Principal Knickerbocker, Will thought: if I want to bake in a sauna, I'll go to a spa!

There was another reason Will was looking forward to the chilly outdoors.

Her dad was going to pick her up in his blue Spider convertible and give her a ride home.

Will loved driving with her dad. He drove really fast—not like her mom, who routinely hit the brakes at *yellow* lights! And Will's dad always let her ditch the seat belt. She would prop herself up against the back of the convertible's passenger seat, and, with the top down, she'd spread her arms and let the wind rush through her shaggy red hair. It felt as if she were off on a grand adventure.

And right now? Will was in desperate need of adventure. Things in Candracar had been pretty quiet, so the Oracle hadn't called on them lately. Not that Will was complaining all that much. Saving the universe from that evil sorceress Nerissa had almost destroyed the girls. Downtime was much appreciated! But every once in a while, she missed the action.

And since Matt Olsen was no longer talking to her, and her mom was constantly arguing with her, Will was spending a lot of that down time with her dad, trying to keep busy.

"My dad . . ." she whispered as she walked down the hall. Those two little words sent a thrill through her. She was still getting used to the idea of having her dad back in her life again.

His return had certainly been a shocker for Will and her mom. One night, he'd simply shown up at their apartment door with presents for Will and a big smile for Will's mom.

Will's mom hadn't smiled back.

With good reason. She was still furious about the fact that he'd abandoned them years ago. She wouldn't even consider patching things up with Mr. Vandom.

Will secretly hoped her mom would have a change of heart. After all, ever since her dad had come back, he'd been nothing but sweet and generous!

Will tried to tell her mom how happy she was having him back in her life, but every time they discussed his reemergence, they got into a fight.

Why does Mom have to be so unreasonable? Will groaned to herself as she thought about some of their most recent arguments. Dad buys me a supercool motor scooter, and Mom won't even let me ride it! That is just *wrong*!

Will's father had eventually bought her mom a gift, too—a beautiful diamond ring. Will wasn't supposed to know about the ring, but she'd been listening at the door when her dad presented it. Unfortunately, her mom had rejected the ring and everything it represented.

Despite all the fun she was having with her dad, there was a part of Will that felt bad about hanging out with him. She and her mom had been getting along really well lately, and she didn't want to cause any friction between them. Plus, Will had to admit she was a little confused. Will trusted her mom, and she had to wonder this: why was her mom so suspicious of her dad? Why wouldn't she forgive him?

Will tried not to worry too much about it, but those prickly little questions lingered. She'd even had a nightmare about her father. It was an awful dream in which she found herself in the middle of a lavish costume party. All the party guests were wearing masks, except Will and her father, it seemed. But when she ran up to him, she saw that he actually *was* wearing a mask. His mask had been carved to mirror his exact features. And when he removed it, Will found herself staring at the blank skin of a face-less man.

Will shuddered. She didn't want to think

about that dream anymore. She wanted to think only *good* things about her dad. He'd missed years of her growing up. Now that he was back, Will was determined to make the most of it.

Quickening her steps through the crowded hall, Will caught sight of Hay Lin and Irma. She was about to call out to them, but stopped herself when she saw the looks on their faces. What's up with them? she thought.

The two girls looked as if they were having a superintense conversation. Hay Lin seemed angry. Irma appeared defeated. They were both standing beside Cornelia's locker, though Cornelia was nowhere in sight.

As Will walked up to them, she overheard Hay Lin say to Irma, "I've seen elephants with more finesse than you!"

Irma hung her head. "I know. I messed up," she replied, staring at the floor. "But I really believe that Jewell knows what he's talking about."

"Jewell?" Will whispered to herself. Who is that? Is she some new girl at Sheffield? Is that why they're so upset? Did this Jewell dis them or something?

There was only one way to find out, Will decided, and that was to *ask*. Plastering a smile on her face, she stepped right up to Hay Lin and Irma.

"Hi, there!" she said brightly. "So, who's this *Jewell*? Somebody I need to meet?"

"Huh?" Hay Lin whipped around. She looked as if she were more than a little flustered by Will's sudden arrival. "Oh, h—hi, Will," she said. "No, uh, Jewell's nobody you need to meet . . . nobody you need to meet at all!"

Glancing back and forth between her two friends, Will noticed that Irma's eyes were glistening. Had she been crying?

"Have you seen Cornelia?" Will asked, deciding to change the subject. "She was around here a few minutes ago."

"Yeah, she was," Irma said distractedly. "But hey, since *you're* here now, maybe I could talk to you for a sec?"

As Irma put an arm around Will, a thought struck her like a forest of falling trees.

How could I be so dense? she thought. I know exactly what Hay Lin and Irma must have been talking about—*Matt Olsen*! It makes total sense. That's why Hay Lin was so flustered when I walked up to her. And Irma probably still feels terrible about hurting my feelings with that stupid "Mandy" song.

"Um . . . if you don't mind," Irma said, "can we talk in private? I've got to tell you something really delicate, and it's about you."

Hay Lin groaned. "Uh-oh," she said. "Here we go again!"

Before Will could ask what Hay Lin meant, Irma was leading her toward one of the side doors. The two stepped outside into the cool, fresh air.

"It's about Matt, right?" Will guessed. "You guys were talking about me and him, weren't you?"

Irma's bright expression fell. "Huh? No! We were just—"

"Don't worry," Will said, waving her hand. "If you really want to know, he doesn't even talk to me anymore."

Sighing, Will took off across the portico that encircled the school as Irma hurried to keep up. She paused between two imposing columns. Stone steps led down to Sheffield's large, green courtyard, where kids were sitting in clusters on the grass or under the large, old trees. But Will didn't notice any of that. Her thoughts were wrapped up in the events of the past few weeks.

As if on cue, Will spotted Matt's baggy red pants and shaggy brown hair. He was standing with his back to her, hanging out with some kids from his band, Cobalt Blue.

Will sighed. "He must still be angry at me because of the scene I made about Mandy," she said out loud.

Irma nodded silently.

Will had already told W.I.T.C.H. about the big Mandy misunderstanding. But she still shuddered at the memory of her awful outburst that night in front of the city pool. She could still see Matt's sweet, easygoing smile—right before she sliced and diced him with her accusations.

At the time, Will had thought that her anger was totally justified. After all, she'd been crushin' on Matt for over a year. They'd worked together at his grandfather's pet shop. They'd hung out with each other and talked about everything. They'd even gone out on what she'd thought were dates. Everything had been going *so* well.

Then Will had had to go on a vital Guardian mission and been forced to create an astral drop—a magical clone that took her place on Earth while she was off fighting evil. In the past, Will had had issues with her astral drop. This time seemed no different. The only difference was that this time the trouble wasn't caused by what the astral drop *did*, but by what she *saw*.

Astral Will had been out one night when she saw Matt hugging a tall girl with long, dark hair—Mandy. The hug was close and affectionate. When the real Will found out, she was convinced that Matt was in love with the girl.

Matt never loved me at all, Will had told herself at the time. He must have thought of me as nothing more than a bud to hang with!

When Matt finally introduced her to Mandy, Will had totally lost it. She'd turned on him, shouting mean things at the top of her lungs. She'd made it clear that she had *zero* interest in being Mandy's—or Matt's—friend.

Matt's puppy-dog eyes had widened in shock. He'd blinked at Will in complete confusion. "I'm sorry, Will," he said awkwardly. "I didn't mean—"

"I know! I know!" Will had cried. "I don't have the right to decide who you hang out with, right? So, fine! Just keep on seeing your little Miss Charisma, but don't think you can force me to spend time with her!"

Will had waited for Matt to shout back, to explain, to say something!

But he didn't.

And the reason he didn't? As it turned out, Will had been completely wrong. Matt and Mandy *had* dated . . . back in kindergarten! Ever since then, however, they'd been just friends.

So where did that leave Will? Feeling like a complete fool, that's where. Matt liked her romantically after all. Or at least, he *had* liked her. Will's insecurities had blinded her to the truth. And her terrible behavior had hurt Matt badly. She'd been mistrustful and nasty toward him, and petty and cold toward Mandy.

It was apparently too much for Matt to forgive. He didn't want to hear Will's apologies or excuses. He'd stopped talking to her completely.

"Don't get offended." Irma's voice broke through Will's dark thoughts. "But I can't say

Matt was totally wrong to be upset."

Will sighed. She shoved her hands down deep into her jacket pockets. "You're right. It was really stupid of me. I keep telling myself that."

"Anyway," Irma said with a little smile, "I didn't want to talk to you about Matt."

Will's eyes widened. "You didn't?" she asked. It was the last thing she'd expected Irma to say.

Irma folded her arms and looked away, as if she were trying to appear indifferent. "I wouldn't dream of sticking my nose in your business."

"Well . . . in that case," Will said, "I'm sorry for misjudging you." She felt silly now. She had been sure Irma was going to confront her about Matt. After all, that *was* the sort of thing Irma would do.

Obviously, I've jumped to the wrong conclusion . . . yet again! Will thought. With a relieved smile, she asked Irma, "So what did you want to talk to me about?"

"About your father," Irma said.

And with those three words, Will's smile vanished.

FOUR

Storm clouds formed over Heatherfield. A frigid wind kicked up, blowing through Sheffield's stately trees. Leaves tore loose from old tree limbs, spinning madly in circles before flying away.

Irma Lair shivered and pulled her coat more tightly around her. *Brrrrrrrrrrr*, she thought. This weather and my friends seem to have a lot in common. They're both bitter, bone-chilling, and unrelenting!

The second that Irma mentioned Will's father, the redhead had turned colder than the wind. Irma had quickly (and obviously unsuccessfully) tried to explain Jewell's warning, but Will hadn't bought it. After an abrupt good-bye, she'd turned her back on Irma and strode stiffly away.

Two strikes, Irma thought. First Cornelia and now Will.

Dejected, she had gone back inside the school to find Hay Lin. Now the two girls were finally ready to go for the day.

"So, Will wasn't thrilled with the news?" Hay Lin asked as both girls exited the building and began walking across the blustery courtyard.

Irma nodded. "You could say that. . . . Yep."

"So . . . what *did* Jewell tell you about Will that got her so upset?" Hay Lin asked a moment later.

"He said that Will shouldn't get too attached to her father," Irma explained, "because he's going to make her suffer."

Hay Lin stopped in her tracks. "Ouch."

"I know," Irma admitted. "The warning about Will's father really couldn't have come at a worse time. Just when things are falling apart between Will and her mother . . . and with Matt."

"Well, Will's reaction doesn't surprise me," Hay Lin said. "Of course she went on the defensive. Her dad's a cool guy . . . at least he seems like one—"

The sound of a revving engine interrupted Hay Lin's words.

Irma looked up. Her gaze followed the direction of the obnoxious noise. Beyond the school's front gate, a sleek blue Spider convertible was pulling up to the curb.

"Speaking of which, isn't that Mr. Vandom's car?" she asked.

Hay Lin nodded. A moment later, the girls saw Will run toward the Spider. She jumped in beside her dad, a big smile on her face. The car's powerful engine revved loudly, and Will's father peeled out.

As they sped away, Irma watched Will lean back against the car seat. The convertible's top was down, and she extended her arms as if she were flying.

Wow, Irma thought, seeing Will's risky maneuver. Doesn't Mr. Vandom care that Will's not even wearing a seat belt? My dad would blow his top if he saw me doing that!

Irma sighed. As the water Guardian, she was usually less rigid and more "free-flowing" about stuff like that. After Jewell's warning, however, she felt almost scared for Will. Something about Mr. Vandom seemed not to be trusted.

Another strong gust blew down from the gathering clouds. Irma shivered again, but this time not from the cold.

I don't think its weird to be worried, she thought. After all, what do any of us really know about Mr. Vandom?

When Will had first moved from Fadden Hills to Heatherfield, she'd come with only her mother. Will had hardly ever talked about life back in her old town. She'd never even mentioned her father or what had happened to him—*ever*.

That sure has changed, Irma thought. These days, Will talks about her dad all the time.

Will told W.I.T.C.H. about their dinners together, their shopping excursions, and all the great gifts he'd bought her. Mr. Vandom had even been going to Will's swim meets to cheer her on—something her mom didn't do!

Irma was cool with Will's new enthusiasm about her father. After all, what kind of water Guardian wouldn't have been able to go with the flow? But sometimes she worried that her friend's excitement might have been preventing her from seeing the truth. And if her dad *was* a problem, Irma realized that the Guardians couldn't just use their powers over the elements to solve it.

"Okay, Irma," Hay Lin declared, interrupting her thoughts. "You've screwed things up with two of your friends. That leaves Taranee."

"Yeah." Irma nodded. "I wanted to get all three over with at once, but the minute the bell rang, Taranee ran off."

Irma shook her head. What's happening to us? she thought. Only a short time ago, we were inseparable—banding together to defeat a dark sorceress. Before that, we fought as a team to rescue another world from an evil prince. Now we can't even find the time to hang out after school! And when we do see each other, it always ends in an argument. Its enough to make a girl go nutty!

"What did Jewell tell you about Taranee?" Hay Lin asked, breaking into Irma's gloomy thoughts.

"He said something really mysterious," Irma confessed. "He said she had a secret . . . and that she'd have to make a serious decision and tell it to the right person."

Hay Lin's eyebrows drew together in worry, and she let out a big sigh.

Hay Lin's right to worry, Irma thought. In some ways, the fire Guardian's situation is even worse than Will's and Cornelia's. Taranee is in an all-out rebellion against her mother, and she's acting like a completely different person. If she has some big, serious secret, I'm scared to find out what it is.

FIVE

Taranee Cook adjusted her thick, round glasses and glanced across the car seat. Sitting behind the wheel, her mother looked prim and polished. Her short curtain of blue-black hair was cut precisely at her jawline. A tasteful string of pearls hung around her neck, and her pale blue business suit looked newly pressed.

You're just the picture of perfection, aren't you, Mother? Taranee thought. No wrinkle would dare appear on your pristine clothing.

Despite her mother's calm appearance, Taranee could see that her manicured fingers were choking the steering wheel. And her brown eyes looked worried as they glanced in the rearview mirror.

Taranee knew what her mother was

stressing about, and it wasn't the traffic. It was her big, awful secret.

"You didn't tell anyone, I hope?" Taranee's mother asked.

Taranee stared hard into her mother's face, trying not to scream.

I don't know why she's acting like she cares about Will or her mother, Taranee thought. The only person she cares about is herself.

Taranee hadn't always felt that way about her mother. She had once looked up to the brilliant, accomplished, successful Judge Cook. For as long as she could remember, Taranee had wanted to be the best at everything—the best student, the best daughter. If she were the best, she would have been just like her mom.

Well, those days are over, Taranee concluded silently.

"Taranee? Did you hear what I asked you?" her mother pressed. "You didn't tell anyone, right?"

"Don't worry, Mother dear," Taranee assured her bitterly. "Your *foul* intentions are safe with me."

Taranee's mom gasped in outrage. The judge wasn't used to having anyone, let alone her own daughter, disrespect her like that. She instantly slammed her high-heeled shoe on the brake pedal.

SCREECH!

Taranee lurched against her seat belt, then back against the seat. Beneath her bright yellow beret, her beaded braid swung back and forth.

"Taranee! What's gotten into you?" her mother demanded when the car had come to a complete stop. "I've never heard you say anything like that before!"

Turning her head toward the side window, Taranee hugged her colorful fabric book bag to her chest and fumed. The bag felt strangely light, and Taranee knew why. She no longer bothered to lug home her usual ton of textbooks.

Finally, she answered. "I've *changed*," she said in a harsh whisper. "Only you haven't noticed one bit, have you?"

Her mother blinked in surprise but stayed silent.

Taranee shook her head in frustration. My mother just doesn't get it, she realized. She probably doesn't even remember the night that started this little war of mine.

Well, I remember what started it, Taranee thought. I remember every word, every look, every detail about that night. . . .

It was the kind of night when everything seemed right with the world. As a fire Guardian, Taranee was used to things blazing out of control. But that night everything was picture-perfect.

Heatherfield's Rock and Roll Café was legendary. It was also one of the coolest, most popular hangouts in the city. And the editor of the school magazine had asked Taranee and Hay Lin to write an article on it!

They would take pictures, sample the menu, and interview the café's owner. But the best part? Taranee's boyfriend, Nigel, had offered to come along to give his opinion. So had Hay Lin's boyfriend, Eric. And before they knew it, the whole outing had turned into a double date of sorts.

Looking back on it, Taranee realized that the night had been ill-fated from the start. Her friends had wanted to go to the café on a school night, and Taranee's mother was superstrict about homework and studying. There was no way she would have let Taranee go.

So instead of asking for permission way in advance, Taranee waited until the very last minute and then placed a rush call to her mom from Hay Lin's place. She told her mom that she had an important assignment for the paper that *had* to get done. She never mentioned that Nigel was coming.

That had been one of her bigger mistakes. Her mom didn't like Nigel. A while back, she'd sentenced him to community service in her own courtroom, and even though his sentence was later reduced, she had never gotten over her image of him as some sort of juvenile delinquent.

Taranee knew better. True, Nigel had once run with a gang of Outfielders (Cornelia's term for those not-so-popular kids who roamed the school looking for trouble). But that was all in the past. In fact, it was because Nigel had left that life behind that the night of the double date turned ugly.

While they were standing near the *closed* café (another problem), they ran into Nigel's former friend Uriah and his sidekick Kurt, who started calling Hay Lin and Taranee names like Metal Mouth and School Nerd. Things quickly went from bad to worse. The police soon arrived, and they were all arrested!

The kids had waited around for their parents to pick them up at the police station. All of them were tense, but Taranee even more so than the others. She knew that her mom had a short fuse, and she *had* sort of avoided telling her the whole truth on the phone earlier that night. But she was not prepared for just how short the fuse would be.

Her mother arrived seething with rage. Her brown eyes flashed with pure fury.

"Let me explain," Taranee began. "I—"

Her mother quickly cut her off. "An article for the school paper, was it?"

Uriah and Kurt were sitting on a bench nearby, and they snickered as Taranee was scolded. Her face flamed red with humiliation.

Then her mom noticed Nigel, slumped on the bench next to them. She gestured toward him. "I should've known *he* had something to do with this!"

Taranee froze in shock. What was her mother talking about? Nigel wasn't to blame. Since he'd started seeing Taranee, he'd completely changed. He took school more seriously, and he no longer hung out with Uriah's gang.

Whatever mistakes Nigel had made in the past were all ancient history. So why couldn't her mother see that? And why couldn't she understand how happy Taranee felt around him?

Nigel valued Taranee for who she was—not for the grades she brought home or the college she would someday get into. He allowed Taranee just to relax and take life as it came. When she was with him, she didn't have to be a superstudent or a superanything. Nigel made her feel good just for being herself.

Unlike my own mother, Taranee thought at the time. I would have given anything for her to be just a little kinder . . . like Hay Lin's mom.

When Hay Lin's mom had arrived at the police station, she was upset about the arrest, but she was also understanding and forgiving. Taranee had witnessed the tender scene between mother and daughter. They had embraced and talked and finally laughed about the whole thing.

Taranee's mom was the complete opposite. Instead of "I forgive you," she said, "I'm ashamed of you." Then she raised her hand high and slapped Taranee across the face.

Tears welled up in Taranee's eyes. The force of the slap had stung, but not as much as the utter disrespect it represented.

Suddenly, something deep and powerful had begun to simmer and boil inside Taranee. The fire Guardian felt rage roar to life inside her.

After trying so hard to be the perfect daughter, she silently fumed, after getting straight As, studying night and day, doing whatever my mother tells me, this is the thanks I get? No patience. No understanding. Just an ugly, harsh slap of humiliation!

For Taranee, it was the final straw. "You shouldn't have done that," she told her mom through gritted teeth. "Not in front of everyone!"

Her mother couldn't see the flames rising up inside Taranee that night. But they were there, burning away every last shred of restraint in Taranee's nature.

From that moment on, Taranee was on strike! Within a week, her homework grades went from straight As to straight Fs. She stopped studying altogether, and she gleefully failed every pop quiz that came her way.

Her mom hit the ceiling, of course. But instead of sitting down and talking with Taranee, she ranted and raved—and then she grounded her. She also began personally picking Taranee up after school and depositing her in a special "study room."

The study room turned out to be her mother's home office, a den lined with bookshelves. Apparently, law books and leather couches were supposed to inspire Taranee to buckle down.

"I went along with being relocated to the Monster's Lair," she told her friends after school one day, "but there's no way I'm doing any homework while I'm in there."

"Then what *do* you do in there?" Cornelia asked.

Taranee shrugged. "Read her legal files, mostly."

And it was doing just that that led to Taranee's learning about the legal action against Will's mother. It hit her in the head—literally—when a file fell off the shelf and onto Taranee. That was how she knew that Will's father was suing Will's mother!

My own mother is going to judge a case that

could affect the life of one of my best friends, Taranee realized, and she never even bothered to *mention* it to me!

Now Taranee's mother leaned back in the car and folded her arms. "The fact that you found that file on Will Vandom's mother in my office doesn't mean that—"

"Don't treat me like I'm stupid!" Taranee shouted. She squeezed her eyes shut, took a deep breath, and turned to face her mother. "You're about to put my friend's mother *on trial.*"

"Oh, come on! I'm a judge. Her file turned up on my desk, and I'm doing my job."

"What a fantastic job!" Taranee cried. "I can't believe you'd listen to all the mean things you hear from Will's dad, a guy you don't know anything about!"

For a moment, Taranee's mother didn't say anything. Then her expression turned furious. She looked as angry as she had the night she'd slapped Taranee.

"How . . . how dare you!" she shouted. "What would you know? You're just a child!"

Just a child? Taranee thought. Just a child?

She has no idea what I've been through or seen. I'm a Guardian! I stopped being a child the minute Yan Lin told me my destiny.

All of a sudden, Taranee could no longer stand being *near* her mom. She turned around and yanked on the car door's handle.

"What do you think you're doing?" her mother exclaimed. "You're not going anywhere, young lady!"

"Try and stop me!" Taranee shoved the door open and swung her legs out.

"Close that door!" her mother shouted. Her voice was high and strained, and her fingers reached out to dig into Taranee's shoulder.

Taranee couldn't believe it. Her mother actually thought she could hold the fire Guardian back!

"Don't!" Taranee warned. Her voice was serious, and her eyes blazed dangerously. "Don't try to stop me, *ever* again. You've got no idea how much I've changed."

Her mother shrank back, and Taranee vaulted out of the car. Letting the door swing wide open, she raced down the street.

The wind was howling. Dead leaves and crumpled papers blew past. The harsh gusts tore at Taranee's open coat, making the red fabric dance behind her like a cape of airborne flames.

Taranee kept running.

I can't take her anymore! she thought, her arms and legs pumping.

Taranee's anger was an explosive force. It seared her with terrible anguish. She didn't know where she was going. She just knew that moving her legs and feet seemed to be the only thing to do.

Eventually, the firestorm inside her burned down to ashes, and her blistering pace slowed. She had no idea what street she was on; tears blurred her vision, and she felt completely lost. Blindly, she pressed forward, wishing and hoping for rescue . . . until a vision stilled her steps.

"I can't believe it," she whispered. She rubbed her eyes to clear them. Then she looked again.

A few boys were gathered near the hearty trunk of a lush, green tree. One of them wore baggy jeans and a familiar smile. His long hair brushed the back of his worn coat collar.

I can't believe it, Taranee thought, stunned by the fateful turn of events. There he was. The boy who made her happy . . . the one who always seemed able to comfort her in her darkest moments.

"Nigel!" she shouted.

Nigel blinked in surprise as Taranee flew to him. A flood of tears spilled from her eyes, and when she reached him, she clung to him, like a drowning girl to a life raft.

SIX

"Do you believe in destiny, Dad?" Irma asked as she sat on the couch, gazing out the living room's picture window.

On the other end of the couch, Irma's father turned a page of the local newspaper. "With the work I do," he said, "I can't afford such luxuries."

"But if you found out it existed?" she asked, facing him. "That your future's already been written?"

He shrugged. "Then I'd try to find out if it could be changed . . . or *re*written."

Irma thought about that. Destiny was something she'd been pondering since the previous afternoon. When a fortune-teller has such major stuff to say about you and your friends, you've *got* to think about it, she told herself.

Hay Lin, Cornelia, Will, and Taranee weren't the only ones whose futures Jewell had predicted. There was a forecast for Irma, too. And it made her wonder about her own past and how much it could affect her future. It made her wonder about other things, too, like . . .

Could a person really change the future? Or was it already set down in permanent ink—like the red pen Jewell had borrowed from Irma to write in his book? Could a person *rewrite* what was already written, the way her dad said?

As the water Guardian, Irma had seen many destinies change in the universe: Elyon's, for example . . .

Elyon Brown had been a friend of Irma's at Sheffield. She'd seemed like your average, normal girl. Only, she wasn't.

Elyon had actually been born a princess in another world, known as Metamoor. But her older brother had taken over the throne and, through force, installed himself as ruler for life.

The loyal servants to the royal family knew that Elyon's brother was evil, and they feared he would harm his baby sister. So, they spirited her away from Metamoor, and hid her on Earth, in Heatherfield, to be exact.

Elyon could have lived out her life without ever knowing the truth about her past. But that was before Irma and the other Guardians found out their true destiny and became W.I.T.C.H. Their first assignment had ended up helping Elyon regain her throne. Now she was the "Light of Meridian," queen of her world.

As Irma considered Elyon's path, she continued to gaze out the living room window. The afternoon sky looked bright again. The clouds had promised a storm, but no rain had ever come. Now the sun was cutting through the clouds, and yellow-white rays quickly erased all signs of threatening gloom.

If the weather forecast can change, Irma thought, maybe the future can, too. After all, W.I.T.C.H. helped rewrite Elyon's destiny. We helped eliminate the dark threat posed by her evil brother. Now her light is shining for her people again.

Irma smiled at that thought and turned back around on the couch. Maybe my dad's right, she decided. Maybe we can *re*write what's been "written" for our futures.

"Good idea," she said out loud. "I mean, maybe the future's written in invisible ink. Or maybe it's written . . . on water."

"What a philosophical discussion," her father said with a chuckle. "Was it that fortune-teller who put all of this into your head?"

Ding-dong!

The doorbell rang, but Irma made no move to answer it.

"I'll get it!" called Irma's mother.

Irma saw her mom walking past the living room toward the entryway. She was dressed comfortably in her favorite copper-colored overalls. They matched her shoulder-length, coppery hair.

From Irma's seat on the couch, she heard the front door open. Unfortunately, she couldn't see who was standing there. She was about to get up and investigate, but then her father distracted her by continuing their conversation.

"You know," her dad said, "yesterday, I heard a bit of chatting back there in the police car." He peered at Irma over the top of his paper.

Irma looked away. "Well . . . um . . ." She didn't want to lie to her dad. "Let's just say Jewell made me think about things," she told him, then quickly changed the subject. "Speaking of which, how's he doing?"

Her father shrugged. "No idea. He disappeared. He didn't show up at the homeless shelter."

Irma didn't like the sound of that. And she liked what her father said next even less.

"The problem is that Mark Zibosky has vanished as well," her dad added. "We had to let him out on bail."

"What!" Irma cried. "Jewell might be in danger!"

Just then, Irma's mom walked back into the living room. "That was weird!" she exclaimed. "A man named Mr. Jewell just stopped by, saying that—"

Irma's dad threw aside his paper and leaped off the couch. Irma was right behind him as he raced to the front door.

"Hey!" cried Irma's mother, jumping out of their way. In their haste, they had nearly knocked her over.

Irma's dad yanked the door open, but no one was there. The front stoop was empty. Irma stuck her head out and looked frantically up and down the block.

Oh, *no-o-o-o*, she thought. Where did he go?

She was about to dash out to look for him, but her father pulled her back. "Wait here," he said sternly. "He couldn't have gone very far."

Irma watched her dad take off down the street. She closed her eyes and thought: please find him, Dad! Please!

"Excuse me!" Irma's mother cried, striding up to the door. "Would somebody please tell me what's going on? Who was that guy?"

Fear and frustration overcame Irma. She turned to her mom. "You should've stopped him! He might've had something important to tell Dad!"

Irma's mother gaped at Irma for a moment. Then she yanked her back inside and shut the door. *Slam!*

"I'm not accustomed to letting strangers into the house," her mother snapped, "or being yelled at by my own daughter. Got it?"

Irma moaned and tightly crossed her arms. "But it wasn't a stranger! It was Jewell!"

"Watch your tone, young lady!" Irma's mom shook her finger an inch from Irma's nose. "I won't allow you to talk to me that way!"

"But it's something really important!" Irma

shouted, ignoring her mother's warning. She was really worried about Jewell. Why couldn't her mom see what was at stake? "That man is risking his life coming here! What's wrong with you?"

"I told you not to talk to me like that!" Now her mom was shouting, too.

"I'll talk exactly as I like!" Irma declared at the top of her lungs.

Her mom looked furious. She put her hands on her hips. "Children don't treat their mothers like this!"

"Right. Their *mothers*," Irma said meanly.

Irma's mom froze. Suddenly, her face fell, and tears sprang to her eyes.

When Irma saw those tears, her own anger dissolved. She hadn't meant to say that, but it was too late now. Her mother was already leaving the room.

"Mom!" Irma cried out. "Mom, I'm sorry! Wait!"

Irma's mother didn't wait. She kept on going, all the way up the stairs and into the master bedroom, where she shut the door on Irma.

Irma couldn't exactly blame her.

Oh, man, she thought. I really am getting

good at the whole foot-in-mouth routine. I didn't mean to hurt my mom's feelings. Anna is the best stepmother I could ever hope to have.

Irma's real mom had died when she and Christopher, her younger brother, were very little. In fact, she didn't remember much about her. Her dad had met and married Anna not too long after her mother's death.

Irma was the flower girl at their wedding. She'd been very young, but she still remembered how excited she'd been that day. Anna had bought her a new dress to wear. It was pink, and the skirt was layered with ruffles. Irma remembered twirling around gleefully, watching the ruffles lift up just over her lower legs like a fluffy, pink cloud.

And that was how she'd felt that day—as if she had been riding a pink cloud of flowers, laughter, and wedding cake. She remembered the tall, bearded photographer. He'd had a hard time getting her to stand still for the group photo.

Her father had finally gotten her to settle down. Then the photo was snapped. It showed the new Mrs. Lair in her beautiful wedding dress, standing beside Irma's dad. He was wearing his nicest suit and holding Irma's baby brother. Irma stood in front of her stepmother's big white skirt, holding flowers and grinning.

That photo still sat on Irma's stepmother's nightstand. And Irma knew she treasured it.

Irma loved the photo, too. It was the very first photo of the new Lair family. It was the very first photo of Irma with her new mom.

Destiny really is a funny thing, Irma thought. It can be full of sadness and tragedy. . . . But then it can turn around and hand you something good. Just look at our family now, and how great things have worked out with Anna.

Wiping her tears away, Irma climbed the staircase. "Mom?" she called, pushing the master bedroom door open a crack. "I—"

Her stepmother's shaky voice called out to her. "Haven't I . . . haven't I always given you everything you needed, Irma? Haven't I. . . . ?"

Irma moved into the room. She saw her stepmother sitting on the bed, dabbing her eyes with a tissue.

"I mean," her stepmother continued, "the fact that I'm not . . . that I'm not your *real* mother . . . Does it . . . Do you . . . ?"

Irma crossed the room and sat down on the bed. "I love you, and you know it," she said softly. Irma put an arm around her stepmother's shoulders. "We both know it."

Anna Lair looked at her and sniffled. Finally, she smiled. Then she laughed and hugged Irma.

"Sometimes I really am a piece of work, aren't I?" Irma joked.

Her stepmother laughed again and nodded. "We all are sometimes. . . . In any case, that man didn't want anything from your dad . . . he wanted something from you."

"What do you mean, something from me?" Irma asked.

"He said he didn't want me to bother you," said Irma's stepmother. "He just left you that book."

Irma followed her stepmom's gaze. A red, leather-bound book sat on the dresser. She rushed across the room and picked it up.

What was going on? she wondered. Jewell was in danger, yet he took the time to come to her house and leave that book?

Omigosh, she thought, flipping through the colorful pages. This was the book Jewell was writing in before he told her about her friends' destinies.

Irma's stepmother crossed the room and put a hand on her shoulder. "He said you'd understand."

Irma shook her head. Whatever's in here must be megaimportant, she thought. "But I don't. . . ." she murmured.

That was when Irma knew it was time to call her friends together. It was time for an emergency meeting of W.I.T.C.H.! Her friends would help her get to the bottom of this . . . she hoped.

SEVEN

This is just like Irma! Cornelia thought. *She* calls an emergency meeting, and *we* end up waiting for her!

Cornelia drummed her fingers on the Formica tabletop. She was sitting at a booth at the Golden Diner. Hay Lin and Taranee sat across from her, looking bored, and Will sat beside her, looking angry. Nobody seemed very eager to hear what Irma had to say.

Including me, Cornelia thought, still stewing about the water girl's big, overflowing mouth.

"How could she be so completely thoughtless?" Cornelia griped, not expecting an answer. "How could she shout about my 'broken heart' in the middle of the main hall, for everyone to hear?"

Will wasn't any happier with Irma than Cornelia was. She told everyone about Irma's advice: *Don't get too attached to your father, because he's going to make you suffer.*

What nerve! Cornelia thought. It's bad enough that Irma told me to start skating again. How dare she say such nasty things to Will about her father!

"Here you go, girls," said the waitress, who appeared at their booth carrying a tray crowded with tall cups; she served them their milk shakes and departed.

Everyone took a sip of their sweet, rich, chilled delight . . . everyone, that is, except Hay Lin. Cornelia looked at her friend quizzically. She wondered if Hay Lin was also mad at Irma. Of the five friends, Hay Lin often ended up in the middle of fights, acting as the mediator. Cornelia did not envy her being in that position! While Hay Lin was usually one of the more sensible of the five, Irma could get under even her skin sometimes. And then, watch out!

Unaware of Cornelia's thoughts, Hay Lin continued to fidget and shift uncomfortably on the seat cushion. Cornelia was about to ask her what was going on when Hay Lin cleared her throat and began to speak.

"Um, guys," she began, "I think there's something you should know."

And then Hay Lin told the girls exactly where Irma's sudden, and nervy, advice had come from. Apparently, Irma had befriended a fortune-teller by the name of Jewell. *He* was the one who'd given her those superpersonal predictions for Cornelia and Will.

Cornelia was stunned. Back at school, she'd yelled at Irma for butting into her business. Yet Irma hadn't really been trying to intrude. It had been this *Jewell* guy. Had she pulled an Irma and reacted without thinking?

"I don't understand," Cornelia told Hay Lin. "Why did Irma tell only *you* about this guy?"

"Yeah!" Will agreed. "It's obviously got to do with all of us!"

Hay Lin sighed. "She thought what he said about me wasn't as heavy as what he said about you guys."

"So what?" Will asked, pounding the tabletop. "We've got a perfect stranger who seems to know all about us! She should have told us! Who is he? Where did he come from? Didn't she wonder about that?"

"She says she knows she can trust him, and that's it," Hay Lin replied with a shrug. "It's just a feeling she's got."

Cornelia exchanged a curious look with Will. "A feeling?" Cornelia whispered. What did that mean? What sort of connection did Irma have with this Jewell person?

At that moment, Hay Lin pointed to the entrance, and Cornelia looked over. Irma had just walked in and was standing there in her hooded coat. Her short brown hair was tousled, and her blue eyes were wide as she nervously glanced around the diner, looking for her friends.

Hay Lin stood up and waved her over. "Okay," she whispered to the others as she sat back down. "I've just told you what's what. You'll have to get the rest straight from the horse's mouth."

"That is, if she finds the courage to get near us," Taranee murmured. She sent Cornelia and Will a pointed glance before adding, "You guys must've been pretty hard on her."

Cornelia could see that the Keeper was feeling badly about misjudging Irma. And, to be honest, Cornelia felt badly, too.

I hate to admit it, she thought, but Taranee's right. I *was* really hard on Irma. I totally took her head off. . . . But I didn't know the truth! I just thought she was being her usual tactless self.

Cornelia's relationship with Irma had always bordered on rocky. Which wasn't surprising—their personalities were practically polar opposites!

Appearances were important to Cornelia. She hated the idea of looking stupid or silly. So she always weighed her words carefully before she spoke.

Irma, on the other hand, was far from cautious. She blew off steam whenever she felt like it. Just like water, Irma's emotions could turn from boiling to icy in a flash.

Cornelia and Irma also had very different outlooks when it came to boys. The water Guardian had never been in love. So she'd never really understood what Cornelia had gone through—and was *still* going through—on account of Caleb.

Caleb wasn't just any boy. Before Cornelia had even met him, she'd dreamed about him. Her dreams had been so vivid that her best friend at the time, Elyon, had been able to draw a picture of him based solely on Cornelia's description.

The thick page from Elyon's sketch pad still sat in Cornelia's drawer, rolled up and tied with a red ribbon. Almost every night, when she was alone in her bedroom, Cornelia untied that ribbon and unfurled Elyon's drawing.

It didn't matter that Caleb had broken up with her and that she *should* have been mad. A part of Cornelia still needed to look at his sad green eyes; his strong, square jaw; his shaggy brown hair; and his dusty rebel coat.

When she gazed at that drawing, every moment they'd shared was made real to her again—the day he'd rescued her from that fountain in Metamoor; their struggle to free his world from the evil Prince Phobos; their fight to stay together time after time (the one fight that proved impossible to win).

Every night in her bedroom she marveled again at the memory of his handsome face and strong form, his bravery and determination. She relived the thrill of seeing his awed expression when he looked at her in her glimmering, Guardian form.

When those memories washed over Cornelia, she was filled with renewed love for Caleb. Once again, she felt their connection.

To Cornelia, Caleb was more than a dream come true. He was someone who had rescued her, in more ways than one—and someone she in turn had rescued. . . .

Not long ago, the evil Prince Phobos had changed Caleb back into his original Metamoorian form—a flower. Cornelia had witnessed the entire thing and had never been more scared in her life. She hadn't known what to do, so she'd just scooped Caleb up in his flower form and taken him back to Earth.

Caring for Caleb became an obsession with Cornelia. She stopped going to school. She stopped seeing her friends. Confused and helpless, she would sit in her bedroom, crying, trying to figure out how to help her handsome young rebel regain his human form.

And what was Irma doing during that particularly nasty period of my life? Cornelia thought, her attention returning briefly back to the reason the members of W.I.T.C.H. had gathered. Irma was making jokes! She laughingly referred to Caleb as Cornelia's "extraterrestrial boyfriend."

After that, Cornelia totally lost it. She threw Irma out of her room.

And ever since then, it had taken all her strength not to throw Irma out of her life completely.

But sometimes, Cornelia now had to admit, Irma wasn't so bad. Occasionally, she even had a few good ideas, like the ice-skating. . . .

At first, Cornelia had been really angry with Irma for even suggesting it. Skating reminded her of the past. Of Elyon . . . and Caleb. Strangely, however, the idea had stuck with her, and when she arrived home that day, she dug her skates out of her closet, hopped on a bus, and rode to Heatherfield's ice rink.

For two hours, Cornelia jumped and spun, raced, and glided across the smooth ice. And slowly, as she moved around the rink, Cornelia began to remember what skating had always meant to her. It had been the one thing that always made her feel strong, alive, and *happy*. Back on the ice, Cornelia felt completely energized. She felt as if she were regaining some magical, lost part of herself. And for the first time in a long while, she began to remember what life was like before Caleb.

"I *can* feel happy without him," she said, sliding and spinning and leaping through the air. "I can feel good . . . all by myself."

Grudgingly, Cornelia had had to admit that Irma was right about the ice-skating—even though Irma had been completely wrong to blurt it out so loudly in the school hall!

Cornelia also had to admit that without Irma, there'd be no W.I.T.C.H., because W.I.T.C.H. wasn't about one girl or two, but, rather, was about the Power of Five, *together.*

In the end, Irma would always be Irma. Maybe they wouldn't always see eye to eye, but Cornelia knew in her heart that they would always be friends.

Cornelia looked up and saw Irma walk slowly over to the booth, her eyes darting nervously back and forth between Cornelia and Will.

"Um, so how's it going?" Irma asked cautiously when she arrived at the booth. "Feel like talking, or do you still want to pulverize me?"

Cornelia met Irma's eyes. She remembered her afternoon, gliding free and happy across the ice . . . and smiled.

"Oh, stop it," she said gently. "Sit down and stop playing the victim. Your milk shake's waiting."

Cornelia slid the tall cup across the Formica table. Irma grabbed it, took a long sip, and slipped into the booth. She exhaled heavily as she sat down, obviously relieved that her best friends weren't going to yell at her again.

Cornelia took a deep breath. She knew she should straighten things out before it got any more awkward. "I have to apologize to you," she told Irma, putting an arm around her shoulder. "You were right . . . about the skating. I took it up again, you know? So I guess you should thank Jewell for me."

Irma's blue eyes widened. "Really?" A smile brightened her tense features. "That means you followed my—that is, *his*—advice!" She was obviously relieved that her secret was out—and that *she* hadn't been the one to let it slip.

"That's just great," Will said coolly, clearly not ready to make amends. "Speaking of this friend of yours . . . Hay Lin said there's something you need to show us?"

Cornelia watched as Irma's face filled with excitement. Typical Irma, she thought. Always hogging the spotlight—when the spotlight was good, that is.

"Check out this book," she said, setting a heavy, leather-bound book down in the middle of their table.

Taranee leaned over it immediately, her natural curiosity getting the better of her. She pushed up her thick, round glasses and examined the binding and pages. "Looks pretty old."

Irma nodded. "Oh, it is. It talks about sea monsters and other mysterious creatures. Take a look at this."

Irma flipped through a number of colorful pages, then pressed the book open. Since she was sitting opposite Taranee in the booth, she turned the book around. Now the fire Guardian could study it right side up.

Taranee stared intently at the open pages. "Why is this picture circled in red ink?" She pointed to an illustration in the middle.

"Jewell did that," Irma informed them. "He was trying to tell me something."

Taranee began to read the text around the pictures. "This paragraph mentions certain aquatic creatures. . . ."

"Aquatic creatures?" Cornelia repeated.

Now she was intrigued.

Taranee nodded. "It says here they're called *water shadows*."

Cornelia drummed her fingers on the table in thought. "Water shadows," she repeated in a whisper. "Irma—any ideas?" After all, Irma was the *water* Guardian!

Irma just shrugged.

None of the other girls knew anything about water shadows, either. Not even Taranee. And she'd read more books than all of them combined.

Cornelia turned Jewell's book back around on the booth's table. She studied the illustration circled in red pen. The picture showed the blue waves of an ocean. Dolphins leaped in and out of the water, and a shadowy figure could be seen just beneath the surface.

"Okay," Cornelia said, "this seems important. And since none of us has ever heard of a water shadow, I guess it's time to get busy!"

EIGHT

Later that day, Cornelia found herself in the perfect place to do a little water shadow research—computer science class. Sheffield's computer science teacher, Mr. Bottlom, had been absent frequently, so she hadn't had his class in weeks. Today, however, a new substitute was filling in for him. His name was Ralph Sylla.

"As I was telling Principal Knickerbocker last night, I can't wait to get to work!" Mr. Sylla announced to the class. "So, take your places at your workstations."

The computer science room was a large, bright space. The workstations were set along the edges of the room—against the walls and the bank of tall windows. There were about twenty kids in the class, and they sat on padded chairs with wheels, in front of computer screens. A few kids had their own computers, but most had to share.

Cornelia waved Will over to a workstation in the corner. "Let's work together, okay?" she whispered. Not only did she want to share her computer with a friend, she also figured they could use the class to do some "extracurricular" research.

Will nodded, and the girls put their heads together in front of the screen. Immediately, Cornelia's fingers began to fly over the keys as she sought out any information on the elusive water shadows.

As the two girls worked, Mr. Sylla put his hands on his hips and surveyed the room.

"Isn't he a dream?" Cornelia heard a girl whisper.

"And to think I never used to like computer science!" her friend whispered back with a giggle.

Cornelia rolled her eyes. Half the girls in class were already crushin' on their new substitute. It wasn't hard to see why. Mr. Sylla was pretty young—in his late twenties at most. He was tall and muscular, with shaggy, light blond hair and intense blue eyes. He also wore a cool little earring, and there was just enough scruff on his chin to make him look a little dangerous.

Every few minutes, Cornelia glanced over her shoulder to check on their teacher. But unlike the other girls, she wasn't crushin' on him. She was worried about him wandering over to her computer and catching her and Will doing their own research.

"Everything okay?" Mr. Sylla asked the kids, as he moved around the room from work-station to workstation. "Using search engines isn't difficult, now, is it?"

"Kid stuff!" one of the boys assured the teacher. "We've been cruising the Net for eons!"

"Speaking of engines, Teach," another boy said, "is that your bike out there?" The boy moved to the window and pointed to a beautiful classic motorcycle outside.

"The old custom?" Mr. Sylla replied. "You bet! I souped it up myself."

Cornelia glanced out the window to see what Mr. Sylla and the boys were talking about. She saw a big motorcycle sitting in the teachers' parking lot.

Will lifted herself up from her chair to catch a glimpse of it, too. "I don't know what to make of the new sub," she whispered to Cornelia, when she had sat back down. "What's his name again?"

"Ralph Sylla," Cornelia replied flatly. "He's charmed the whole class, but I'm not falling for his act."

Will raised her eyebrows questioningly.

"There's something about him I don't like," Cornelia explained. "He's been glancing over here way too often."

"Well, the important thing is that he not bother us during our search," Will whispered.

Cornelia couldn't have agreed more. She continued looking among the Internet search engines—the ones she knew about, anyway. She tried every keyword combination she could think of . . .

Water Shadows
Shadows in the Water
Jewell (and) Water Shadows
Ocean Shadows
Aquatic Creatures

"It's useless," Cornelia said at last. "I can't find any sites that talk about water shadows!"

"Water shadows, huh?" Mr. Sylla said.

Cornelia froze. A few seconds ago, the teacher had been on the other side of the room. Suddenly, he was standing right behind Cornelia and Will, staring at their computer screen.

Cornelia turned nervously to face Mr. Sylla. He didn't seem angry or upset that they weren't doing their assigned research. In fact, he was standing there *smiling* at them.

"You guys interested in sea monsters?" he asked.

Cornelia glanced worriedly at Will. What do we do? she wondered. What do we say?

Will took over. "Um . . . do you know what they are?" she cautiously asked the teacher.

"Sure!" Mr. Sylla replied. "Just a second."

He walked over to his desk and grabbed a pen and notebook. Then he returned to Cornelia's and Will's workstation.

"Every legend has some truth behind it, you know," he said as he scribbled in the notebook. Then he tore out the page and held it out to them. "Here are a few sites that might come in handy."

"Um . . . thanks," Cornelia said warily. Why was Mr. Sylla helping them? Shouldn't he have been lecturing them on their classroom responsibilities or something like that? But when she looked over his big, bold handwriting, her eyes widened in surprise. "Looks like you're pretty well informed about the subject."

Mr. Sylla shrugged his broad shoulders. "Well, the fact is, I surf random sites pretty often. And, between you and me . . ."—he winked—". . . mysteries are my hobby!"

Cornelia furrowed her brow.

Mr. Sylla's acting a little too curious about what we're searching, she thought. Isn't his behavior a little . . . *strange*?

She exchanged a questioning glance with Will.

Will simply shrugged.

Okay, maybe he is just trying to be helpful, Cornelia thought. *Maybe* . . . but that "mysteries are my hobby" comment is just plain weird. I can't see any other teacher saying something like that!

Cornelia swiveled her chair around to face the computer keyboard again. There seemed to be more to their new substitute teacher than met the eye. For now, however, she'd have to let her suspicions go. Class would be over soon. If she wanted to search all the sites the teacher had given her, she'd have to start typing right away!

NINE

When classes were over for the day, Hay Lin found a sunny spot in which to sit in the school courtyard. Irma and Taranee soon dropped down next to her, talking and laughing.

The grass felt soft, and the sun was warm. It was the best weather Heatherfield had seen all week, and it lifted Hay Lin's spirits. The air was sweet and warm, boosting her mood even more. The harsh winds of the last few days had wreaked havoc on the air Guardian. It felt great to breathe in the air of the fine day. Too bad the reason they had gathered wasn't so light and breezy.

Jewell's red book was spread open in front of Hay Lin. Taranee had read it. And Cornelia had glanced through it, too. Now it was Hay Lin's turn.

Flipping through the pages, Hay Lin had to admit she wasn't quite sure what she was looking for.

Maybe I'll see something the other girls have overlooked, she told herself. But then again, studying any type of book has never been my strong suit, so that seems doubtful.

Before long, she heard Cornelia's and Will's voices. Hay Lin looked up to see the two girls walking across the courtyard. She held her breath when she saw their long faces. Hay Lin was not up for bad news.

"Find anything?" she asked hopefully.

Will sighed. "Not much. And what we did find was kind of confusing."

Will and Cornelia sat down on the grass, forming a circle with the other Guardians. Cornelia tossed back her long blond hair. Then, with an official air of authority, she pulled a small stack of papers out of a binder.

She began to read from them in a crisp, practical voice. "When speaking of certain shadows, one is most likely referring to beings endowed with magical powers . . . in some way comparable to elemental spirits—"

"Elemental?" Hay Lin interrupted. "You mean, like us?" Of the five friends, Hay Lin had always thought of herself as the most comfortable with her connection to nature. Maybe because, like air, she could flow, or perhaps it was because she was a second-generation Guardian. Either way, it made complete sense to her that the water shadows were connected to elements.

Will nodded, taking over for Cornelia. "Yes, these magical shadow creatures are connected to the four elements—water, fire, earth, and air," she explained. "Except these spirits are *made up of* their particular element. Those of fire are made of fire, those of air are made of air, and those of—"

"Wait a sec!" Irma cried. "You're talking about creatures that don't have real bodies?"

"More or less," Will said. She took the papers from Cornelia and quickly flipped through them. Then she read out loud: "*Water shadows, for example, are practically invisible to the naked eye . . . although some fishermen have claimed to have seen them in the middle of groups of dolphins. They look like fast-moving shadows, with an almost human form."*

When she stopped reading, Will passed around one of the pages, explaining how she and Cornelia had downloaded the report from a Web site on seafaring legends. A picture on the page showed a fishing boat out at sea. Depicted were two fishermen standing on the deck, pointing to a group of dolphins. In the midst of the dolphins, a phantomlike shadow floated eerily just beneath the surface of the blue waves. It looked just like a man!

"Reminds me of those stories you hear about fishermen seeing mermaids," Taranee noted as she examined the picture.

"That's exactly right," Will said. "They say the stories about mermaids came about because of these sightings of water shadows."

Irma looked stunned for a moment, sitting on the grass. "Beings that *live* in the water and are *made* of water?" she murmured. Then the water Guardian rose up on her knees, her blue eyes full of excitement. "Incredible!"

Cornelia shook her head. "Not incredible. *Impossible!* I mean, we're on Earth, not in Meridian!"

Irma stared in disbelief at Cornelia. "Why

can't magical creatures exist here, too?"

"Because I use my logic to reason," Cornelia snapped, "and not my imagination."

"But *we* exist, don't we?" Irma pointed out.

Hay Lin was in complete agreement with Irma on that one! Frankly, she couldn't see why Cornelia wasn't, too.

"Oh, please!" Cornelia cried, throwing up her hands. "You guys, talk to her! I give up!"

Will turned to face Irma. "So, tell us, then," she said, her tone patient but firm, "what do you think your Mr. Jewell wanted to say to you by pointing out these water shadows?"

Hay Lin exhaled in frustration. Why are they ganging up on Irma? she wondered as she continued to page through Jewell's red book. The last thing W.I.T.C.H. needs right now is another big fight!

If only they'd had something else to focus on besides the water shadows business, she thought. Faster and faster, she turned the pages of Jewell's book, hoping something might jump out at her—some clue the others might have overlooked. Then, suddenly—"Omigosh!" Hay Lin whispered. "What's this? Look!" she cried loudly. The bickering stopped as the startled girls turned to face her. Hay Lin smiled. "Maybe. Jewell wanted us to find *something else!*"

"Like what?" Irma asked.

"Like *this*." Hay Lin held up the slip of paper she'd found. "It was between the pages of the book."

Taranee took the piece of paper from Hay Lin. "It's a check-out slip from a library."

"Now we're talking!" Cornelia cried. She snatched the check out slip from Taranee and waved it under Irma's nose. "Here's something *real* we can investigate! Better than legends."

"Okay, okay," Irma said. "But what's the plan?"

Cornelia examined the slip. "By discovering who checked this book out," she said, "maybe we'll find Jewell, too."

"No *maybe* about it!" Irma exclaimed. "We've *got* to find him, because he's in danger! Mark Zibosky is looking for him, and—"

"Yeah, yeah, Irma, you told us already," Will reminded her. "We understand how serious the situation is. But that doesn't mean the guy doesn't still owe us an explanation."

Now I get it! Hay Lin, thought. Now I see why Will and Cornelia are giving Irma so much attitude. The actual idea of a water shadow existing doesn't concern them. They just want to find this Jewell guy and figure out how he knew so much about *their* personal lives!

Hay Lin didn't blame them for being so touchy. If the predictions he had made for her hadn't been so rosy, she might have been giving Irma a hard time, too!

So it was decided: they'd go to the library. Hay Lin slipped her purple messenger bag over her shoulder and stood up. The rest of the girls grabbed their coats and backpacks, and all together they headed for the library. It was time to find out just who had checked out the book—and why.

The main branch of the Heatherfield library wasn't far from Sheffield Institute. It was housed in an old, historic building made of granite. Tall, arched windows lined the front, along with potted plants and a large stone statue of a winged angel. The girls climbed the steps and entered the building's marble lobby.

When they stepped into the reading room, quiet enveloped them like an invisible cloud. Hay Lin could practically hear the crush of the carpet beneath her shoes as they all moved toward the librarian's desk.

Row after row of heavy bookcases lined the main aisle. Like mahogany giants, the dark bookshelves rose up toward the top of the ceiling twenty-five feet above them. Hay Lin was awed by the sight of the thousands of volumes.

It reminded her of the Guardians' recent trip to Meridian to visit Elyon, whose palace also had a vast library. Only, the books in Elyon's library were written in a language Hay Lin couldn't begin to understand.

Hay Lin marveled at the prospect of not only learning a new language, but also reading books about a foreign world. That was exactly what Elyon would be doing for the next few years of her life . . . that and ruling her world as its new queen!

"Come on," Cornelia urged the girls, breaking into Hay Lin's thoughts. "I think I see the librarian."

Hay Lin continued to follow Cornelia and the other Guardians down the main aisle of the library reading room. Once the girls arrived at the front desk, Will approached the librarian. Cornelia was right beside her, and Irma and

Taranee stood behind them. Hay Lin hung back, her attention flitting from one bookshelf to another. She was still wondering how anyone could ever read all those books when the sound of Will's voice brought her attention back to the situation at hand.

"Come on . . . please?" Will begged.

Hay Lin noted the urgency in Will's voice. It looked as if she were getting into an argument with the librarian.

"I'm sorry, I can't help you," the woman told Will. "I'm not authorized to disclose that kind of information."

Will shook her head. She leaned over the librarian's desk and pleaded again with the woman to help her out.

"I'm sorry," the librarian repeated. "It was very kind of you to bring this book back, but I *can't* give you the address of the person who checked it out."

As Will continued to negotiate, Hay Lin regarded the librarian. She was an older woman with light hair gathered up in a high bun. Behind her cat-eye glasses, her brown eyes were alert and intelligent, and her face was creased with lines that made her look very wise. She was—it appeared—the quintessential librarian.

The woman's wrinkles and the way she spoke—in a voice that was firm but kind—reminded Hay Lin of another familiar figure: her grandmother, Yan Lin.

Immediately, Hay Lin's thoughts drifted out of the library, back to her childhood. Every evening, while Hay Lin was growing up, her grandmother told her bedtime tales. There were stories of dragons and emperors, as well as colorful mountains and magical princesses. In a way, her grandmother was "keeper of stories."

Hay Lin smiled to herself. I suppose the librarian is the keeper of stories, too, she thought as she glanced at the thousands of volumes surrounding her.

It was from her grandmother that Hay Lin had learned of her destiny as a Guardian. And then she had learned that her grandmother had once been a Guardian as well. Suddenly, all those bedtime stories took on brand-new meanings! They were not just fairy tales but real stories about the Guardians' history.

Sadly, Yan Lin had passed away. She was no longer a part of Hay Lin's earthly life. Now she resided in Candracar, with the Oracle, but sometimes Hay Lin dreamed of her. And when she visited Candracar, she got to see her as well.

Hay Lin's thoughts of her grandmother were interrupted by a frustrated sigh. Apparently, despite Will's puppy-dog eyes and major amounts of pleading, the librarian was refusing to give them the name of the last person who'd checked out Jewell's book.

The girls moved away from the librarian's desk and gathered together a few steps away. Irma shook her head. "Talk about sea creatures," she whispered. "Are all librarians this crabby?"

No one seemed to know what to do next. They'd hit a roadblock in their journey. Then Hay Lin smiled. I know what to do, she thought.

Every member of W.I.T.C.H. brought something unique to the team. The courage of the Keeper, the fire Guardian's temper, even the water Guardian's flowing emotions could be helpful in a crisis. And tenacity wasn't a bad thing, either. The earth Guardian's stubbornness often helped the girls get a job done. But through their various adventures, they'd learned that when a brick wall stands in front of you, simply knocking your head against it does nothing but give you a bump on the head.

"Sometimes, my little one," Hay Lin's grandmother had once told her, "you must know when to rise up, above the road you're on, and find another path. . . ."

Yan Lin's words were very simple, yet very profound. They reminded the air Guardian of exactly what *she* contributed to the team.

"Have you noticed how stuffy it is in here?" she whispered to Irma. "What do you say we open the window?"

With another smile, Hay Lin closed her eyes and connected to the ancient energy deep inside her.

"Air . . ." she said in a hushed voice.

Outside the library, invisible forces in the atmosphere began to swirl together in a soundless stream.

Whooosh!

A stiff breeze assaulted the window near the librarian's desk, blowing it open with tremendous force. The swinging window frame slammed the back of the wall as the rushing air swept inward. Papers flew off the librarian's desk and scattered all over the room. It looked like a tornado of paperwork!

"Oh, my!" the librarian cried. She quickly scuttled over to retrieve the papers.

Taranee's and Irma's mouths opened. Will and Cornelia shot Hay Lin a look of amazement, followed by an expression of thanks. With the librarian totally distracted, the Guardians could sneak over to her desk and access the records on her computer!

Will pulled Cornelia over to the keyboard. There, Cornelia typed the title of the book into the system's search engine.

"Found it!" she softly exclaimed. "The last person to check out this book was a Benjamin Crane."

Will leaned in closer to the screen. "Thirty-four Achaboud Street," she said, reading Crane's address. "What are we waiting for? Let's get a move on!"

Will and Cornelia raced ahead. Irma and Taranee were right on their heels. On the way to the exit, however, Cornelia stopped and looked back over her shoulder.

"What is it, Cornelia?" Will asked.

Cornelia frowned. "Nothing . . . it's just . . . just a funny feeling." Then she shook her head. "C'mon! Let's get out of here!"

Hay Lin followed the others, wondering what Cornelia was worried about. Then she got a funny feeling, too—as if someone were watching them.

Glancing back, she stifled a gasp. Their substitute computer science teacher, Mr. Sylla, was there in the library. He had just stepped out from behind a bookshelf near the librarian's desk, and he had a very odd expression on his face.

Did he see that little stunt I just pulled on the librarian? Hay Lin wondered. She couldn't be sure, and when she turned to take another look, he abruptly ducked down to retrieve some papers from the floor.

Shrugging, Hay Lin turned around again and headed for the exit. Outside, she found Irma waiting for her with her arms crossed.

"What?" Hay Lin asked, seeing Irma's smug smile.

Irma lifted her chin in the direction of the open window. "It's not like you to do that kind of stuff," she whispered.

Hay Lin shrugged. "I did it for a good cause.

You said yourself that Jewell might be in danger."

"You're right." Irma nodded as a smile tugged at the corners of her mouth. "So? What are we waiting for? Let's go."

TEN

"What a creepy place," Irma announced. "If my folks knew I was here right now, they'd totally freak!"

The girls had had to look at a map to find Benjamin Crane's address. And when they'd finally found it, they had let out a collective gasp of disgust. Thirty-four Achaboud Street was located near Heatherfield's industrial port, in the "bad" part of town.

Yikes, Irma thought, as she and her friends stepped off the city bus, this place could use a little redecorating.

The concrete sidewalks were cracked and crumbling. Abandoned buildings stood dark and empty. Windows were broken, and graffiti was scrawled along the dirty brick walls. Immense warehouses and grimy smokestacks towered over everything else. Gulls cried and machinery rumbled as giant cranes unloaded steel containers from a huge freighter. And even though it was daytime, the whole place felt dark and claustrophobic.

Irma could feel the tension among the girls as they walked down the cracked sidewalk. When they reached the corner, Cornelia stopped to look at street signs. There were a number of roads splitting off at the intersection.

Will raised an eyebrow as she looked up at the signs. "I'm surprised they gave the streets in this area real names."

"That's still not saying much," Cornelia noted. "Listen to the names. Kraken Avenue, Bourbon Alley, and . . . ah, there it is!" Cornelia cried excitedly. "Achaboud Street!"

Irma wasn't nearly as excited. When she looked down the street where Benjamin Crane was supposed to live, she shuddered. "Just when you think you've seen the *worst* of it!"

The girls headed down the street—only, it was so narrow and shadowy that it felt more like an alley. Finally, they came to the address. It belonged to a broken-down wooden building.

The entire structure looked flimsy, and the dingy outer cement walls needed a patch job badly. Three big packing crates were stacked near the steps leading to the front door.

Ugh, Irma thought. Somebody should call that show that does home makeovers—this place is in desperate need of some tender, loving care!

As the girls drew closer, they saw a brand-new metal gate surrounding the yard.

That's odd, Irma thought. Everything else is so run-down, but the gate is new. I wonder what—or who—Benjamin Crane is trying to keep out? Lucky for us, the gate's open. Or maybe not so lucky. I guess we'll have to ring the doorbell to find out!

The girls passed by the crates and climbed some shaky steps.

"No bell," Taranee noted, when they stopped in front of the door. "What do we do, knock?"

"No, just blow," Irma joked. "Seeing how run-down this place is, the door's bound to fall right off its hinges!"

Just then, as if in answer to Irma's threat, the door's hinges squealed, and the weathered slab of wood creaked open. A big man appeared in the doorway and stepped forward. He pressed his face up against the dirty screen door.

"Yes?" said the man through the screen. His voice was deep and gravelly.

"Um, hi, there!" Taranee said. "We're looking for a Mr. Benjamin Crane."

"That's me," the giant replied. "What do you want?" The man's gruff voice seemed full of venom, and his meaty hands were balled up in fists.

At the sight of the bald giant, Irma recoiled, her heart racing. While dark sunglasses hid the man's eyes, there was something familiar about him. . . .

Wait a second! I know this man, she realized. He's not Crane! He's one of the thugs my dad arrested the other day! When he caused trouble in the station house, Rose had to use her martial arts skills to keep him from escaping.

Irma's eyes narrowed dangerously. "I'll tell you what we want," she told the thug. "We want you to get out of our way, for starters!"

In a flash of fury, Irma reached deep into her being. She felt powerful magic roiling there, as if the heat of her temper had boiled a deep, underground river. Then, as she raised her hands, a crackling blue force streamed through her body and out of her fingertips. She directed the energy straight ahead of her, and in a burst of blue fire, the screen door exploded.

S-BAAAM!

"Aaaagh!" the man cried as he was sent flying backward.

Breathing hard, Irma quickly withdrew her magic. She put her arms down and stood with legs braced. Behind her, she could hear the other Guardians' alarmed gasps.

"When you said you wanted to knock the door down," Will said with a nervous laugh, "I thought you were kidding!"

Taranee shook her head, looking through the giant hole in the screen. "What was that all about?"

Irma gritted her teeth and clenched her fists. "That's not Benjamin Crane!" she told her friends. "That's one of Mark Zibosky's men!"

And if Zibosky's men are here, she added silently, I hope that Benjamin Crane *isn't*.

Stepping through the hole in the screen door, Irma entered the building, with Will,

Cornelia, Taranee, and Hay Lin close behind. They moved down the hallway. At the end of it, they found the bald thug who had confronted them sprawled on the floor.

Cornelia put her hands on her hips and looked down at the man. "So if this thug isn't Benjamin Crane, then who is he?"

Irma groaned. "That's what I wanted to ask him!"

Will bent down to check him out more closely. "I don't think we're going to find out anytime soon. He's out cold."

Irma knew the clock was ticking. They didn't have time to worry about the knocked-out thug. They needed to find Crane. Leaving the hallway, Irma started searching the place. The interior was in slightly better shape than the run-down exterior. The walls were flimsy but newly painted. There were curtains on the windows and framed pictures on the walls, all of them depicting either sailing ships or seascapes.

Irma continued to look through each room until she heard a strange, muffled noise. Following the sound, she headed into one of the back bedrooms.

That was when she saw him. "Mr. Jewell!" she cried.

Irma instantly recognized the man's weathered, wrinkly skin and long white hair. And evidently, he recognized her! His bright, blue eyes lit up when he saw her. Unfortunately, he couldn't respond. Someone had tied him to a chair and put a gag in his mouth!

"Mmmmf! Mmmmf!" mumbled the old man.

Irma rushed over and untied the handkerchief gagging him. "Do you feel okay?" she asked. "Is everything all right?"

The old man smiled at Irma. "Yes. Thank you, dear!" he said in a kindly voice. "But . . . I'm not Jewell."

"What?" Irma gasped.

He licked his dry lips. "My name is Benjamin Crane."

Maybe the thug had hit Jewell on the head, and now he was suffering from an odd case of amnesia, Irma thought.

Though she had a million things to ask him, she didn't press. Instead, she helped him to his feet and then, slowly, guided him back into the main room.

She found the rest of the Guardians there, tying up the man who had been knocked out earlier. He was still unconscious, but they weren't taking any chances. They'd lifted him into one of the chairs in the room and secured his hands and feet with twine that they had found in the room.

"There, have a seat," Irma told Benjamin Crane, gesturing to a large table in the middle of the room. He nodded and took a seat in a wooden chair at the head of the table. The other girls greeted him as they settled around the table.

Before she took her own seat, Irma found a small fridge in a makeshift kitchen one room over. She filled a pitcher with water and brought out a glass for Jewell—or Crane—to drink.

Wow! He must be thirsty, Irma thought as she watched the man finish his glass in two big gulps.

"Thank you again, dear," he said as he set the glass down.

Irma nodded. "No problem."

It looks like I'm going to have to get this conversation rolling, she thought. After all, it was my run-in with Jewell that brought us here.

As quickly as she could, she explained to the man how they'd found him. She told him about meeting Jewell, and about the book and the library slip. Then she asked *him* something. "Who are you, exactly?"

"Well, as I told you, I'm not Jewell. My name is Crane. I'm a fisherman," he replied proudly. "It's my job. My life."

Irma's eyebrows rose. Well, she thought, that certainly explains the man's weathered, supertanned skin! Fishermen faced the sea and wind for days, even weeks at a time without a break. But that didn't begin to explain the whole Jewell look-alike situation.

"Everything started around six months ago," Crane continued. "I was sailing off of Lighthouse Cape, and the weather was taking a turn for the worse. My boat was in bad shape, but I needed to keep fishing."

Irma nodded. As Crane told his story, she could almost see the raging ocean. During a storm, the wind and waves could be brutal. The relentless surf could capsize a boat or batter it to bits on the rocks near shore. And as the water Guardian, she knew just how powerful a force the sea could be.

"The waves got choppier and choppier," Crane went on, "and soon I was taking on water. I remember going into the sea. It was freezing cold!" He shuddered. "So dark and merciless! Terrible!"

Irma glanced around the table. The other girls were staring wide-eyed at Crane as they listened to his frightening tale.

"I tried to swim to shore," he said. "The lighthouse was shining out from beyond the waves, telling me that safety was right there, within my grasp. . . ."

"Did you make it?" Irma asked.

He sadly shook his head. "I'm not a young man anymore, and the current spares no one. I started to go under . . . when suddenly something lifted me up. A mass of swirling water started to carry me off toward shore."

"Swirling water?" Cornelia repeated skeptically.

"Oh, yes!" he told her, nodding excitedly. "At first, I thought it was a dolphin . . . because I saw some dolphins jumping around in the water not far from me. When I got to the shore, I found I was so exhausted I couldn't even climb up on dry land. It was then that I felt two hands grab me and pull me to safety. And then . . ."

Irma leaned forward. "And then *what*?"

Crane's blue eyes were bright. Even now, he seemed to be reliving the memory. "And then I saw it! With each turn, the lighthouse cast its beam on an extraordinary being."

"A being?" asked Will. "What *kind* of being?"

"A sort of . . . *shadow* . . . with a vague outline," Crane replied. "The image became more defined, and then the creature took on my own appearance. It told me not to be afraid, and it carried me here to my home."

As Crane's words began to sink in, Irma felt her heart begin to beat faster. Is he saying what I think he is saying? Lifting herself from her chair, she put her hands on the table and leaned toward the old man.

"You're talking about—"

"A water shadow! Yes! A legendary being!" Crane's head bobbed. Then he sighed, as if in resignation. "And to think that, before then, I'd never believed in old sea stories."

Suddenly, everything clicked into place. "So this shadow . . ." Irma said. "You're saying that he's the fortune-teller? He's—"

"The shadow didn't have a name," Crane interrupted. "So when I recovered, I decided to call him Jewell."

Irma looked around the table. In one glance, she could see that the girls were having very different reactions to the fisherman's story. Hay Lin seemed to believe him. Taranee looked doubtful, and Cornelia and Will looked the most skeptical of all.

Well, I'm not one bit skeptical, Irma thought. I believe every word that he's saying!

As the water Guardian, Irma knew that her belief didn't come from her head. It came from somewhere else, a place deep inside . . . an ancient well, where her elemental power lived.

To her, believing in the power of a water shadow wasn't a matter of trust. It was a matter of magic!

ELEVEN

Will drummed her fingers against her thigh. She liked the old fisherman. He seemed nice enough, and he'd clearly been through a terrible ordeal. But that didn't mean she had to believe everything he said. In fact, the trauma he'd experienced meant she should question him *more*, right?

"After he saved me, and I named him Jewell, his predictions started coming," Crane was saying. "Jewell showed me all the places where I'd have good luck fishing. And did I ever! Business started going so well that I had to buy a new boat."

Will glanced around the kitchen. She noticed that the sink was really old, but the fridge was brand new. The table-and-chairs set they were all sitting at looked new, too, yet the roof appeared to be leaking. The whole place was like that—filled with broken-down stuff alongside brand-new stuff.

Obviously, the old guy has recently come into some money, Will silently deduced. I'll buy *that* part of his crazy story.

"Jewell didn't ask me for anything in return," Crane went on. "He just wanted to see me happy. He was like an angel . . . who came from the sea."

"Then what happened?" Irma asked. "Where do Zibosky and his thugs fit in?"

"Well, you see, some of Mark Zibosky's men noticed my sudden good luck. They started getting nosy. And it wasn't long before Zibosky himself discovered my secret . . . that I had a genuine fortune-teller living with me. He thought Jewell was my brother. So he took me hostage and started to blackmail him."

Irma thought she grasped Zibosky's plan. "Predictions about the near future, in exchange for your life?"

Crane heaved a big sigh before continuing. "Zibosky used Jewell's predictions for his shady dealings . . . illegal betting and trafficking.

Finally, there was the police raid and—"

"Hold on! Wait a sec!" Cornelia interrupted. "I don't mean to be disrespectful, but even you'll have to admit that this story sounds a bit . . . fishy."

A *fisherman*'s story sounding *fishy*? Will nearly laughed out loud at Cornelia's "corny" pun. For some reason, though, Irma didn't see the humor in the situation. Her expression grew dark and troubled.

That's got to be a first! Will thought. Irma's usually the *first* one of us to make a joke in a tense situation.

Instead, the water Guardian pounded the table. "I believe him, Cornelia!" Irma shouted. Then she turned to the old man. In a much softer voice she said, "I'm sorry, Mr. Crane. We—"

"At least you listened," the old man said with a shrug. "Just believe me when I say I'm *not* crazy. I've found all sorts of information about water shadows. I took out books from the library, did research. . . . I discovered that these creatures have special powers, including clairvoyance. They can even change form, although once they've changed"—then he shook his head sadly—"they're no longer able to change back."

Will folded her arms. Irma was glaring at the Guardians now, almost daring them not to believe Crane's tale.

Fearing Irma's attitude and Cornelia's skepticism was going to lead to a major argument, Will quickly suggested they step outside for a little privacy.

After reassuring Crane that they would be right back, the Guardians put on their coats and filed out the front door. Before she could leave, Will noticed that Crane had stopped Irma. He whispered in her ear, and then, with a smile, let her go.

They descended the steps and gathered behind the crates outside the house. The weather had gotten chillier, and a breeze blew down the alley from the nearby docks. Will shivered and shoved her hands deeper into her pockets.

"I know what you're thinking, guys," Irma told them, starting off the discussion. "But the guy in there *isn't* Jewell!"

Will shook her head. "How can you be so sure?"

As Irma stepped up to Will, the Keeper of the Heart could almost feel her friend's emotions pulsing in the air. Irma was filled with worry, fear, and anger about Jewell's fate.

"If you'd seen Jewell's eyes, back at the police station, you'd understand," Irma said. Her voice was pleading, almost desperate. "He knew I was the only one who could help him. Don't you get it? He can't change back to his original form. The man in there is sad, true, but there isn't the same desperation. You have to believe me."

Will was silent for a long moment. As Irma's words sank in, the breeze from the ocean became stronger. It encircled her with tangy scents of salt and sea.

Will had to admit, she'd been skeptical about the Jewell thing from the start. The other day at school, when Irma had tried to tell her something about her "future," she'd angrily brushed it off. She knew that Cornelia had been just as angry about Irma's butting into *her* business. But Irma was only trying to help her friends. She was trying to watch their backs. And wasn't that what W.I.T.C.H. was supposed to be about in the first place?

We may have control over the elements, Will thought, but our real power all along has been the power of friendship.

Irma didn't need skepticism from her fellow Guardians just then, she needed them to step up and back her; to step up and *believe* in her. That was what the Heart of Candracar was for—and that was why Will was going to use it.

Will raised her eyes to meet Irma's. "If Jewell's in trouble, then what are we waiting for?" she said with determination. "Let's go find him."

"Wait!" Cornelia cried. "Wait just a minute!" She turned to face Will. "You seemed pretty skeptical before—at least as much as I was!"

"Yeah, Will," Irma agreed. "What made you change your mind?"

"Simple." Will smiled at Irma. "I've never seen *his* eyes, but I saw the look in *yours*."

"You *believe* me?" Irma asked.

Will nodded. "Even though you sort of blundered through this whole thing—"

"*Blundered*?" Irma protested. "Hey! That's not fair!"

Will laughed. "You're right. I guess I just

realized that you were trying to help all of us, and it came from the heart. So I think it's up to the Heart to return the favor."

Closing her eyes and stretching out her palms, the Keeper silently called to the Heart of Candracar. The ancient crystal rose up within Will, pulsing with power from its ethereal source. Like a tiny blazing sun, it appeared, floating in the palm of her open hand.

"Did Crane say where we could find Jewell?" Will asked Irma.

"Lighthouse Cape," she replied with a grin. Her blue eyes were bright with anticipation.

"You're sure?" Will asked.

Irma nodded. "Seems he spends whole days there out by the lighthouse. The problem is that Mark Zibosky knows that, too."

"Okay, then," Will said, focusing on the Heart, "I think that calls for transposition. Brace yourselves, 'cause we're outta here!"

And, in a blinding flash of light, W.I.T.C.H. was gone.

TWELVE

Special Agent Ralph Sylla's steady blue gaze never left the front door of the house on Achaboud Street.

He'd been following Will, Irma, Taranee, Cornelia, and Hay Lin since they'd left the school grounds earlier that day. Now he stood in the chilly shadows, waiting for them to reemerge from the broken-down building.

He flipped up the collar of his trench coat, checked his watch, and frowned. They'd been in there for at least forty minutes, and he was beginning to worry.

This part of town was notorious. Criminals and gangsters operated openly. It was not the usual hangout for straight-arrow students. "So what could they be doing here in this sleazy place?" he mused, to no one in particular.

He'd heard about a police raid in the neighborhood a few days before, and he also knew that Irma Lair's father was a cop. He suspected there might be a connection. And connections were the name of the game in Sylla's business. For the past few months, he had been making connections between these girls and some odd occurrences.

Before going undercover to observe the girls, Sylla had consulted with Agents Medina and McTiennan. Like himself, they were detectives for Interpol. Sylla's interest in these five girls had been piqued when he had read Medina and McTiennan's files on the strange disappearance of a Heatherfield girl named Elyon Brown.

The Brown case was closed now. But Elyon's best friends happened to be the same five girls who were later listed as eyewitnesses to some very odd happenings in the seaside resort area of Green Bay. The police report alone had raised the hairs on the back of Sylla's neck.

The report had made mention of lightning

strikes that split trees, monstrous beings that roared with fury, and beautiful winged fairies.

Whether these girls had had anything to do with those supernatural happenings, Sylla was not one hundred percent sure . . . *yet*. But he was determined to find out. That was why he'd gone undercover as the girls' substitute computer science teacher. Sylla was ready to observe for himself what these girls were up to on a day-to-day basis.

Luckily, he had happened to "overhear" something about their latest interest—water shadows. Then he had spotted them at the library and followed them from there to the docks.

So, *what* exactly are they looking for down here? he wondered. And why did they go into that building?

He'd watched earlier as Irma Lair had extended her arms and somehow *attacked* the building's entrance. The force she'd used was incredible. It had blown a giant man backward. Sylla still remained puzzled about how she'd accomplished that!

Now, many minutes later, the door opened again, and Sylla watched as the girls filed back out through the damaged screen door.

Okay! Here they are at last, he thought. Where are they going next? Sylla watched closely as they walked down the rickety steps, and—

The agent's fists clenched. The girls had disappeared from view! They'd stepped behind a wall of stacked packing crates, and he couldn't see a thing!

"It's okay," he whispered to himself. "They're sure to come back out again in a few minutes."

Heaving a sigh, Sylla waited for them to emerge. As the minutes passed, however, he grew more impatient. He ran a hand through his shaggy blond hair. "They've been behind those crates for way too long," he rasped. "What are they up to?"

Suddenly, a dazzling light flashed from behind the crates, and it wasn't some weak photo flash or headlight beam. This light was searing, almost blinding in its intensity.

"What the . . . ?" he whispered.

Sylla was dying to rush over and see what was happening, but he held himself back, not wanting to blow his cover. After ten minutes, there was still no sign of movement, so Sylla slowly drew closer to the building and carefully peeked around the corner of one crate.

"It . . . it can't be!" he cried. "They've really disappeared!" He looked up and down the alley. There was no sign of them. Yet he'd been watching the crates the entire time!

"There's no way those girls could have walked away from this site—not without my seeing them!" he said aloud. So how had they escaped? And more importantly, where had they gone? "If this isn't a mystery," he whispered, "then my name's not Ralph Sylla."

As the special agent walked away, a tiny smile made the edges of his lips turn up.

I may have lost the girls today, he thought, but there's always tomorrow. After all, what I told Cornelia and Will was *almost* true. Mysteries aren't just my hobby, they're my job.

THIRTEEN

Irma's eyes flew open, and she gasped. They had made it to Lighthouse Cape! She and the other Guardians were now perched at the top of the lighthouse that gave the place its name. Gusts of wind blew Irma's auburn hair around her stunning face. But she barely noticed. She was too busy examining her Guardian getup. Even after all the times she had done it, turning into a Guardian still sent a thrill coursing through her.

The power of the Heart had totally transformed her. She was no longer a short girl with chubby cheeks. Her limbs had grown longer and stronger. Her features had matured into those of a gorgeous young woman. And her lean, strong body was clothed in striped tights, a purple skirt, and a belly-button-baring turquoise top. Glimmering wings sprang from her back.

Dragging her attention away from her upgraded outfit, Irma looked around. The Guardians' surroundings had gotten an upgrade, too! Gone was the dark alley near Crane's house. Now, far below Irma, jagged rocks emerged between white-capped waves. The surf was rough, brutally pounding the shoreline.

Suddenly, something else caught her eye. She'd spotted Jewell! He was running across the beach, with Mark Zibosky and his men close behind.

"There he is!" Irma cried, pointing Jewell out to the other Guardians. They could see that Zibosky and his men were quickly catching up to the magical water shadow.

"We're not going to do anything to you," they heard Zibosky shout at Jewell. "We just want you to tell us what the police asked you!"

But Jewell kept running, finally racing into the lighthouse and slamming the door shut behind him. But it didn't stay closed for long.

SBRAAAAANG!

Zibosky and his thugs broke open the door as they chased Jewell inside.

"Up there! On the stairs!" Irma heard one of them shout.

As the men climbed the interior staircase of the lighthouse in pursuit of Jewell, Irma and the other Guardians got ready. There was no way they were going to let Zibosky and his cronies hurt the man.

The afternoon sun was still strong as Jewell raced outside and onto the deck that encircled the lighthouse. From their position, the Guardians saw him frantically look left and right, seeking a way to escape.

"There you are at last!" Zibosky shouted, when he appeared on the deck a moment later.

Jewell stopped and turned. Irma could see his kindly, wrinkled face and bright blue eyes. They were full of fear! There was no escape— only a narrow balcony ahead of him. And beyond its low metal railing was a terrifying plunge to the sea below.

Irma watched as Zibosky closed in. He looked the same as he had at the police station . . . only a tad scarier and a little less suave.

Zibosky laughed cruelly as he grabbed Jewell; his voice was just as cold and hard as Irma remembered it from the day he'd threatened her dad. But, luckily for Irma, he hadn't noticed her or her friends. They stood pressed up against the lighthouse, waiting. Telepathically, she told her friends to take care of the other guys. The water Guardian would deal with Zibosky.

"Your twin, Ben Crane, didn't want to tell us where you were!" Zibosky shouted at Jewell. He shook the old man by the lapels of his tattered green coat. "But we know how to make people talk. And we know how to make them shut up, too!"

"You know," Irma loudly interrupted, "I always figured only gangsters on TV shows used cheesy lines like that."

"What? What the . . . ?" Zibosky looked up to see Irma standing on the balcony rail, her wings glittering in the sunlight.

Irma grinned—but not at Zibosky. "Hi, Jewell!" she said. "I'm happy to see you!"

"Me, too!" The fear in Jewell's face melted away as he returned Irma's smile. "I *knew* you'd show up!"

Zibosky was not as pleased. He stepped

behind Jewell, putting the old man between himself and Irma. At the same time, he wrapped one of his strong arms around Jewell's neck in a choke hold.

"D—don't move!" Zibosky growled. "Don't get near me!"

Irma rolled her eyes at the thug's attempt to get tough. It was a pretty lame effort, too, given that he was stammering in fear!

"Take it easy, Zibosky," Irma warned. "You don't want to make me angry, do you?"

Zibosky narrowed his dark eyes as he looked at Irma. "Mike! Orlando!" he yelled over his shoulder.

"Are you calling your thugs, by any chance?" Irma asked the man. She gestured toward the balcony's doorway.

Zibosky turned his head and gasped.

Cornelia, Taranee, and Will stood there, with Hay Lin fluttering above their heads, her long black pigtails billowing in the sea breeze. Irma knew that for someone not used to seeing magical creatures, the sight was probably terrifying.

And Zibosky had every reason to be terrified.

Irma's fellow Guardians had stepped out of the shadows and knocked his henchmen out cold. Mike and Orlando were now imprisoned in cloud bubbles.

"Too bad for you!" Will called to Zibosky. "My friends and I are used to capturing much bigger gorillas!"

Irma laughed as she jumped down from the railing and started to approach the criminal.

"Wh—who are you?" Zibosky demanded, his deep voice laced with fear. "Wh—what do you want!"

"We just want you to leave Jewell alone," Irma replied.

Zibosky glared at Irma with a mixture of fear and fury. His gaze shifted to the other Guardians. Will, Cornelia, Taranee, and Hay Lin were moving toward the railing, closing in on him!

"Stay away!" Zibosky shouted over the howling ocean wind. In fear and panic he started inching backward. "Don't come any closer!" he threatened.

"Look out!" Irma warned. The man was moving straight toward the railing.

But Zibosky wasn't listening. He was too

busy trying to escape. Suddenly, his legs hit the lower railing, and he fell over backward, taking Jewell with him!

Irma lunged, reaching toward the falling men. But her fingers closed around only one wrist—Mark Zibosky's. Jewell continued to fall, plunging toward the breaking surf below.

Irma reacted instantly. There was no way she could physically grab Jewell—not while he was falling so fast and her other hand was holding on to Zibosky's wrist, so instead, she lifted her free hand and called forth the water energy living deep inside her. Instantly, crackling lightning jumped from her open palm in a blinding streak.

Tears of fear sprang to her eyes as the energy caught up with the falling Jewell. "Please," she whispered desperately, "please let this work. . . ."

As Irma watched her bolt of energy close in on the falling Jewell, the other Guardians crowded around her, looking down. Suddenly, they all gasped.

Jewell's human form disappeared before their eyes. And then, into the surf below fell the unmistakable outline of a man made of *water*.

Irma had done it! She'd given Jewell what he'd asked for. She'd freed him from his earthly form and returned him to his watery home.

He was back in the vast, blue ocean . . . where he belonged.

And better yet, Irma and the others were where they belonged, too, doing what they did best—making the world safer.

IRMA HOPES IT'S TRUE THAT JEWELL IS REALLY A MAGICAL CREATURE IN HUMAN FORM.

BECAUSE THE ONLY WAY TO SAVE HIM NOW IS TO CHANGE HIM BACK TO HIS NATURAL FORM . . .

. . . TO SEE TO IT THAT WATER . . .

. . . RETURNS TO WATER.